MW00903281

Switching Lanes

Switching Lanes

and Other Stories

PAUL UCHE

Copyright © 2015 Paul Uche
All rights reserved.
ISBN: 1512191124
ISBN 13: 9781512191127
Library of Congress Control Number: 2015907960
CreateSpace Independent Publishing Platform
North Charleston, South Carolina

Reviews

Deeply touching...

A clear voice

Exudes authenticity and sincerity.

Takes the reader around the globe.

Smart, engaging and emotionally resonant..

Deft, playful, youthful use of language

Acknowledgements

A GOOD NUMBER of the stories in this collection were put together or updated by Paul in the hospital while he was facing the reality of his battle with leukemia. As we publish the work on Paul's behalf, the Uche family wishes to thank all those who supported Paul through this tough time. You helped make this work possible.

Paul had a big heart, and nothing shows that more than the diverse network of people he closely connected with throughout his life and throughout the world. If anyone is not mentioned here, we apologize. Just as he did, we love you all.

Mrs. Mona Nashman-Smith: You've loved Paul from the moment he first showed up seeking a place in your school. When he won awards at ABA, your pride in him shone as brightly as did ours. You made that long trip from Muscat to Toronto to spend several days to support Paul in the hospital. You have been and remain a great friend to the entire family. We can't thank you enough.

The entire ABA staff and students in Oman: You were there for Paul well before his trials. You were solidly behind him throughout his struggles. You have now been one of the strongest pillars for the Paul Uche Memorial Foundation. Thank you.

Dr. Mina and Meredith Ghattas: From the moment Paul showed up in Cambridge to pursue his education at MIT, you accepted and treated him like a member of your family. His last Thanksgiving dinner was with you. He always spoke fondly of the two of you, never failing to emphasize how "cool" you both were. Thank you for being Paul's parents in Boston and wonderful friends to the Uche family.

The Sigma Chi fraternity: The bonds Paul forged at MIT as a member of the Sigma Chi fraternity are unbreakable. The laughs were constant; the smiles, infectious; and, most importantly, the desire to see each other succeed, unquestionable. The many trips you all made from various corners of the United States to Toronto were something Paul looked forward to and thoroughly enjoyed. We are grateful to all of Paul's Sigma Chi brothers too numerous to mention.

Michael Gibson and David Rodriguez: as Paul's roommates and best friends, you hold a special place in Paul's heart and a connection that death cannot break.

Obinna Okwodu: you were Paul's little brother and now Bernie's too.

Alyssa Muskett, Rachel Fraunhoffer, Bari Rosenberg, and Brittany Sullivan: You were the leading ladies that Paul always talked about. Your support for Paul in sickness and health truly touched us all. You remain his sisters, and we love you all.

Dr. David Avigan and the Feldberg team at Beth Israel Deaconess Medical Center in Boston: thank you for the fantastic care you gave Paul.

Katelyn Trainor and Hannah Yarmolinsky: thank you for treating Paul more like a friend than a patient.

Kristen MacDonell of Princess Margaret Cancer Center in Toronto: thank you for your friendship, which Paul looked forward to and enjoyed every day.

Mohamed Yousif: You've been one of Paul's best friends since you two were thirteen years old. You've been through it all. It brought him joy that he was able to see you almost every day in Toronto. From Oman to Canada, you've been a constant presence. We are glad that you were an integral part of Paul's life, and we hope to be the same in yours.

Obinna and Chioma Udora: As Bernie and Paul's oldest childhood friends, it is refreshing to know that there are people you can always count on. Your support and love warmed Paul's heart, and we appreciate your lifelong friendship.

Mohaned Kheir: You became Paul's favorite. During his hospital stay, you brought a sense of normalcy to Paul's life. Every day you made him smile, and that's all he ever wanted. Paul once said that if he left Toronto, he would miss you greatly. That speaks volumes to the strength of the friendship you both forged over a short period of time. For that we will forever be appreciative.

Other Toronto friends of Paul and Bernie, too numerous to list: Paul cherished your love and the many hospital visits, and we thank you immensely.

Ifeoma Okwuosa, Tobore Agbaire, and Aunty Dorothy: You neither knew Paul nor our family before we moved to Toronto. You fell in love with Paul, cheered him on, and became pillars of support for him and our family. Thank you immensely.

To all who organized bone-marrow drives and all who came out in droves to get swabbed for Paul: you not only stood up for him, but your selfless acts will surely save other lives.

Reverend Wendell Gibbs and members of First Baptist Church Toronto: thank you for embracing Paul and our family without asking questions.

Dr. William Schreck: You lovingly reviewed every story in this book—a very delicate assignment when the author was no longer around to be interacted with. Thank you also for supporting the family in many ways.

The board members of the Paul Uche Memorial Foundation - Mrs. Mona Nashman-Smith, Prof. Ogwo E. Ogwo, Prof. Kalu Ogbureke, Sheik Muhammed Marhuby, Engr Emmanuel Ukandu, Engr. Ben Amanambu, Mazi Chukwu Igwe Chukwu, Michael Gibson: thank you for all the work you have already done to permanently honor Paul's memory.

Robbie Zein and Jan van der Meijden: you were the rock and still are.

Family members and family friends all over the world, too numerous to mention: thank you for your steadfast love, prayers, and support.

We hope you all enjoy Paul's work on the pages that follow.

Dedication

To a world without prejudice, even if it is just a small world within the known world.

Foreword

Like the accomplished commuter…students
are able to travel competently through life;
and, ultimately, they will be able to pass on
their own wisdom in a natural way to those
who come after them.

—HOWARD GARDNER

WRITTEN FROM THE perspective of a young adult, the
principal purpose of *Switching Lanes* is to share the genius insights and creative energy of a Renaissance man.

Paul Uche was a gifted writer, a successful scholar, a creative musician, and a fierce opponent on the basketball court. In this book, he uses the past and the future as creative sources to connect memory and fantasy about living, and in doing so he delivers a compelling and insightful series of short stories, and accompanying blogs, to awaken the conscience of each reader to the importance of embracing all that life has to offer—the good, the bad, and the ugly.

Paul's writing explores the inner landscape of love, courage, and failure. His short stories emerge as life's lessons. In Paul's words, "Nothing compare[s] to exposing the public to a genuine experience." Paul takes his readers on a heartfelt journey; each short story captures his passion for faith, love, sports, friendship, and his Nigerian origins. His writing showcases the authentic journey of life's challenges, which every reader can relate to in one way or another. Again and again in this book, we are reminded of Paul's words about his struggles with leukemia: "Life is a funny beast that throws a lot of curveballs at you."

Paul lost his life to his most formidable opponent, leukemia, in June 2014 at the young age of twenty-three. In *Switching Lanes* Paul writes, "Sometimes you have to go somewhere with no map and no planned destination...I finally extracted myself for the slow pilgrimage home." Ironically, these words have come to define Paul's last days with us.

While his friends and family mourn the physical loss of this brilliant Renaissance man, Paul will live on immortalized in his writings, his music, and his influences on all who knew him and loved him.

Finally, Paul was the epitome of a "lifelong learner." Hopefully, this book will inspire others to write and share their "own wisdom...[for] those who come after them."

God bless you, Paul. May you rest in peace.

Mona Nashman-Smith

Editor's Note

B EFORE WE DIVE in ....

Paul blogged extensively while he was battling leukemia.

Two of his posts seem like the natural introductions to this collection of his short stories.

In *Creative Juices* Paul announed the start of the brave effort that yielded many of the stories.

His final blog post, *The Aggressive One,* introduces us to Paul's unwavering optimism, even in the face of extreme trial, and to his positive outlook on life - the recurring themes in the stories themselves.

On June 19, 2014, Paul lost his valiant fight against leukemia, but in addition to his short stories, he made sure to leave a huge collection of songs he wrote and produced himself. Some of his lyrics follow the short stories, together with more of his blog posts.

Creative Juices

Hello, everyone,

When I was treated the first time around, I had school to keep me mentally focused. I was stimulated each day by working toward graduation. Now that I have my degree, I am a big believer in the idea that now can be a time to push myself in new ways. I don't want to sit idle in the hospital, so I am looking to expend creative energy. Finishing up my mixtape *The Dissertation* was a part of this drive.

The Dissertation itself started from a commitment to writing and recording one song each week. I released them on Wednesdays, and this practice allowed me to get better as a rapper. Now I am challenging myself to put a short story together every week. I can't promise that you'll love my work—who reads anyway?—but I hope to learn from the experience.

With my academic and professional pursuits on hold, there is no better time to become a triple threat: engineer, writer, and rapper! I want to be able to justify introducing myself as "Paul Uche, Renaissance Man." I kid, but on a weekly basis, I hope to post a link to a short story of mine. I am hosting them on wattpad.com for now. Feel free to fawn, fret over, or help me fix anything I write.

The inaugural story is a piece called "The Twenty-Four-Hour Shot Clock." The story is about a high schooler who takes the big championship basketball game into his own hands.

To give you a quick update on how things are going, today is day nineteen, and my ANC and blood counts are all near rock bottom. I have not been sick for a while, so I am happy about that. A lot of people have been getting swabbed, and bone-marrow drives have been taking place as well. I am humbled by the response.

Love,
Paul "Renaissance Man" Uche
September 4, 2013

And then, his final blog post...

The Aggressive One

Hello, everyone,

I am to undergo another round of chemotherapy tomorrow. The goal is the same as last time: to kill the leukemia cells responsible for my respiratory complications.

I have been talking about my lung issues for a very long time. Since I have also been nursing three or so fevers a day, the decision has been made to attack the leukemia in a very aggressive fashion.

There is a good chance that the aggressive chemotherapy, a rarely used protocol, will be tough to endure. Tomorrow I will have one-to-one nursing, where a nurse will stay with me and monitor how I cope with the treatment. There are concerns about my heart, blood pressure, and the plethora of side effects associated with chemo. One of my doctors asked me a few times whether I was sure that this is what I want to go through. At twenty-two years old, I am young, and I still believe that I will return to full health. The only other choice would be to enjoy palliative care at home.

I won't lie. Things don't always play that simply in my head. I don't want to give you the impression that I mentally bulldoze through everything. I am a jar of maladies. I have been in the hospital for more than three months, and no one talks about remission from chemotherapy anymore. I hurt most days and often in new ways. I thank God that I do arrive at my optimistic outlook.

After this round of chemotherapy, so long as I am completely stable, I will be moving to Ottawa to perform an experimental transplant. I could not get strong enough in time to participate in the trial in Toronto.

Wish me luck.

Best regards,
Paul "Looch" Uche
November 2013

Contents

1

The Twenty-Four-Hour Shot Clock

THE GYMNASIUM WAS awash in silence as Coach sprang off the bench and made a T with his hands to motion for a timeout.

The opposing team broke into a chorus of whoops and sloppy chest bumps. Heads bowed, and brows furrowed. Coach's ragged unit dragged their feet to the bench. Their ten-point lead had been eviscerated in a matter of minutes, leaving them trailing by the slenderest, the most precarious of margins. Coach gazed at his clipboard, a clipboard that mocked him with its blankness.

"If these plays don't work, just throw bombs," he had always huffed.

He gave dramatic speeches at the beginnings of games and then plopped down on the bench to mull over other things. In his fine gray suit, with his clean-shaven face cupped in his supple hands, he looked as out of place as he behaved. A benchwarmer piped up to keep him informed of each game's proceedings.

During the course of this particular season, one he had hardly paid attention to, his squad had become a Cinderella outfit. All of a sudden, the entire school embraced them, and the rafters were swollen with people in school gear that still smelled like department stores. This game, the championship game, was the first to commandeer Coach's attention; as a recently divorced high-school history teacher, he had not thought about basketball enough to be able to conjure new ideas to reverse the game's momentum.

Coach recited a couple of lines about "heart" and "hustle." If a Hollywood story were to be made about his underdog team, the script would have to be rewritten in order to address all of the clichés. Coach knew there was only one person he could trust among the dread-infested gawkers that puddled around him. He clapped John, his captain, on the shoulder and breathed, "I want a bomb."

The boys nodded sheepishly, and John gave a smirk and a wink that was only intended to inspire himself. He was on the brink of a scene that every boy prepares for in gyms, parks, and driveways. He had amassed a portfolio of mock game winners, all made while friends counted down from ten to zero and, with the ball in the air, mimicked the sound of a buzzer going off. This was a high-school destiny more fulfilling than becoming prom king.

Almost everyone on the team accepted that, each game, fate hinged on the flick of Johnny Bomb's wrist. He looked as if he should be catching waves in California instead of traipsing up and down the court. Still, with the ability to bench press more than double what any of his teammates could, with his long blond hair that sashayed around his Alice band while driving to the rim, and with the latest pair of Lebrons strapped to his feet, he made for a convincing hero. He was the gunslinger who dared to shoot from any distance and any angle at any time. His desire to earn his moniker was insatiable, but whether he scored or not, he flashed his dimples, knowing he would be back at it moments later.

There was only one person who rejected Johnny Bomb as deity. He was the team's point guard, Chinedu, and he teetered on the edge of taking matters into his own diminutive hands.

The would-be renegade known as Chinedu trudged back onto the court, swimming in both his uniform and his thoughts. He noted where other players were on the court, especially those a couple of inches away. He knew he would receive the inbound pass and be expected to charge into a forest of trees. He would need to draw attention in order to safely swing the ball out to Johnny for one of his patented bombs.

The stat tracker, a basketball enthusiast utterly incapable of catching a ball or a tan, would grant him the assist. Unlike the Oscars, the best supporting actor would not receive his just due. Chinedu grimaced at the sight of Johnny, who, with confidence made out of Teflon, flashed his dimples.

Over the final minutes of the final quarter, the other team had figured out the home team's handful of plays, denying them at every twist and turn. Johnny had gone ice-cold, building a house of bricked shots. No matter. Coach still grunted, "Bombs," every couple of minutes, even as the other team chipped away at their lead like a sculptor in a hurry. Coach seemed to think that the word could have the same effect as saying, "Shazam."

As the whistle blew and the players littered the court once more, the crowd found its lungs and started chanting, "Johnny Bombs! Johnny Bombs!" MacKenzie, the prom queen elect, was the loudest of them all. The past two minutes of shot-making futility had been lost to a sudden onset of amnesia.

Johnny clapped his hands repeatedly as the ball first came to Chinedu, fulfilling part one of the prophecy. The clapping made the rebellious point guard's teeth grind. Over the course of the season, Chinedu's father had almost broken his jaw clenching his own teeth at the same sound. "That boy claps his hands like a maniac, and you just shovel the ball to him. He gets the ball even when he is double-teamed or facing the other way or missing the basket entirely. I bet if the monsters from *Space Jam* took away his basketball skills, you would still pass him the ball. What do you do all of that practicing for if you are going to play so mindlessly?" his father had wailed. He had too much melanin to go blue in the face, but he almost did anyway.

As a quiet kid, Chinedu struggled to wrestle his father's attention away from work. When Papa Chinedu came back home in the evenings, all he wanted was a cold beer and silence to concentrate on watching the news. He called every pundit a Muppet. He was a sports enthusiast too, but his allegiance to basketball had gone with Michael Jordan. He cared more about soccer, but Chinedu had never been able to will his feet into doing his bidding to play the beautiful game.

Now there was no one in the crowd for Chinedu to claim as his own. With the ball in his hands though and the clock ticking down to zero, all eyes belonged to him. The world knew that Johnny was supposed to get the ball and gave little credence to Chinedu's meanderings.

He then made his script-busting move.

———

Vishal hustled over to set a futile screen. Just as spindly as Chinedu but half a foot taller, he was routinely brushed aside. Chinedu crossed over to his right hand and plunged into the heart of the painted area. His defender did not pretend to follow him and lurched faithfully toward Johnny. The defender's arms flailed in the air to deflect any pass headed his way. Despite being doubled, Johnny clapped as if he were looking to knock the skin off his hands.

Chinedu's insides twisted as he picked up his dribble and took two steps toward the basket. He stretched out a wobbly arm toward the rim, and the ball, nestled in his palm, felt heavy. Number twenty-one, a freak of nature on the opposing team, rotated over and obscured the basket like an eclipse. Nine times out of ten, the six-feet-eight-inch colossus would have spiked the shot like a volleyball. He was caught flat-footed though, because he had not expected the invasion. Number twenty-one could only claw at Chinedu's wrist, and the subsequent slap rang throughout the gymnasium. Chinedu's headband flew in one direction as he crumpled the other way. The buzzer blared as his shot flirted with the rim before rolling away. Chinedu lay motionless on the ground, biting his lip to hold back a well of tears. His best defense against an outbreak of anger was to remain where he was. He could hear the patter of the ball, but not the squeak of sneakers, the groans of defeat, or the yelps of victory.

"Foul on number twenty-one. Two free throws for number three," the referee finally said. The other players were already lined up side by side to corral the rebound if necessary. The referee quickly waved them away though. "No need to line up. There's no time left on the clock."

Johnny Bombs looked like a kid who had lost his lunch money to the school bully, as he made his way back to the bench. Coach stood up and glared before putting an arm around his dejected superstar.

Chinedu took his place at the foul line. He was the game's sole survivor. He slipped his headband back on and performed his patented free-throw routine: one bounce, bend your knees, three bounces, exhale, pause…fire alarm.

⁂

There had been no advance notice about a fire drill. In fact, the principal, who was up in the rafters, was more confused than most. A nervous exodus ensued. In time, the whole school had power walked outside, and the students milled about in the parking lot. Coach and his team waited together in uncomfortable silence.

"You better not miss," Johnny groaned intermittently while pacing up and down.

Coach thought the same, as a newfound desire to win the championship edged out the anguish of his failed marriage. Coach had struggled to take to Chinedu because the young man oscillated between being a wallflower and a know-it-all. Coach wanted to respect how much Chinedu practiced and consumed the game of basketball, but when you are a man trying to wing it as the coach of an irrelevant team, having a player who regularly threatens to show up one flaw or another in your underdeveloped tactics is a nuisance. "Are you ready?" he asked.

"Yes, Coach!" Chinedu yelled.

Coach was bemused because he saw no signs of knobby knees clapping together or nails being chewed to pieces.

Chinedu could barely wait to get back onto the court. He wanted to achieve the relevance he had always sought. He envisioned bringing the trophy home to his father, declaring, "I won the game!" His mind had not yet stopped to think that he could miss.

The other team filed into their bus and left. The referees got into a white Toyota Camry and followed suit. Chinedu wanted to pull them all back with a lasso, but they were hardly to blame. No one wanted to remain outside under the sweltering sun.

"We can all go back inside. Someone pulled a fire alarm," the principal huffed.

There was a wave of relief, but Coach and his team stayed huddled and confused. Principal Smith was a stout man and visibly upset about the running around he had been called upon to do.

"The game is delayed though," he added. "The referee is gone. The other team left too. So every student must go back to class."

Chinedu wondered why they needed the other team at all when he was there, the gym was full of basketballs, and any person could attest that he made two shots in a row. They could even record it on their iPhones if proof was needed. The decision was final though, and Chinedu was not one to remonstrate. His mind had not yet stopped to think that he could miss.

Coach dismissed the team. He had not smoked on school grounds since he himself had been a student over twenty years ago, but the thought began to ravage his mind. Miss Fisher was filling in to teach his class, so he decided to spend the rest of the day doing something more ill-advised than smoking. He talked himself into visiting his ex-wife.

Judith Albright, formerly known as Judith Thomas, was likely to be home. She was a writer and a painter with an apartment brimming with easels, canvases, buckets of paint, and an assortment of paintbrushes. Books, manuscripts, and papers covered every surface that a human could possibly sit and write at. Judith's fingers often looked like a coal miner's, and most of her T-shirts were freckled with a rainbow of colors.

Whenever Coach tried to make fun of her, she jabbed back, "At least I am passionate about things." He was prone to lamenting about how redundant his life felt. "All I do is teach the same old stuff year after year," he barked. Judith nodded automatically and seldom looked up at him unless he had something positive or novel to say. Then she would perk up, sweep her chestnut hair aside, and pay rapt attention.

The brand new suit and the newly leased BMW would startle her. Coach had bought them in a bid to reinvent himself.

The math teacher at the school, who was two years older than him, looked like Usher. Math Teacher Usher – MTU (as Coach had heard the students call him) turned their female colleagues into the gossiping high-school students whom they taught. "Just because I'm forty and know a lot of calculus doesn't mean I can't look fresh, my man," Usher chirped. He had a reputation for being a slow grader when the truth of the matter was that he didn't spend a lot of evenings at home bent over a mountain of illegible, crumpled sheets of paper. The man was far from in a rut, so

Coach, living alone again for the first time in a decade, tried to follow in his footsteps.

Still, he'd been as listless and unmotivated as ever until the championship game. Judith had to be impressed that he had developed a passion for coaching high-school basketball. He pictured her throwing her paintbrush aside and smiling wonkily at his efforts. What did it matter that his passion for the team had only sprouted with no time left on the clock? He would invite her to watch Chinedu shoot the two free throws the next day. He just hoped that the kid's confidence would hold out.

Chinedu normally enjoyed MTU's lectures and found calm in their structure. The differential of x^2 was $2x$—always. Comparing and contrasting, in four thousand words, the American lifestyle as presented in *The Great Gatsby* and in a modern novel of his choosing had been his biggest headache until then. As a Nigerian, it had felt slightly irrelevant to him. He wanted to read Chinua Achebe, Wole Soyinka, and Chimamanda Ngozi Adichie. He would have drawn up a longer list of desired Nigerian authors, but he did not know of anyone else. He was a rudderless child of the diaspora. When he scoffed at home about writing his literature essay, Papa Chinedu scolded that he better take his studies seriously or else he would not be accepted to a university in America, adding, "Do you want to be sent to Nigeria for university?" Chinedu rarely had a response that was suitable for deployment. Papa Chinedu hissed and turned back to listening to Wolf Blitzer. Nigeria was an effective threat. .

Chinedu could not be convinced that a paper that only one person would ever read was more important than the free throws he was to take. At any future high-school reunion, no one would come up to him and say, "I remember that analysis of *The Great Gatsby* and Book X that you wrote—you know, the one with the weak conclusion. Such a shame." On the other hand, they would be quick to point out, "You turned into Shaq, missed two shots at the line, and cost the whole school its best shot at a first city championship."

Chinedu sat in the back of the classroom in his oversized uniform, but his classmates exercised no subtlety in steering their eyes his way. Many adults would say that the basketball game was just that, a game. History would surely not be so kind in its summation of events.

Math Teacher Usher seemed to be talking to Chinedu. Chinedu saw his mouth move, but the sounds remained unprocessed. He looked into a pair of eyes that were tucked behind thick black glasses that could often be found perched on faces in hipster enclaves. Usher's skin was surprisingly void of creases, a testament to his routine trips to The Body Shop. Chinedu tried to read the face as if he were Professor X, to no avail.

"I'm sorry, Mr. Wade. I didn't hear the question."

"Focus, Mr. Ojimba. I hope you can do that when the time comes to hit those free throws tomorrow!"

Chinedu watched the clock on the wall, and his heartbeat fell in sync with its ticking. Despite sitting at the back, he was the first one out of the door when the school bell belched. His usual stride was a languid yet concentrated ode to possessing swag. He made for the school bus, looking to sit in the back with his headphones blaring so that he could cut himself off from the growing babble about basketball. When he stepped onto the bus, he saw a gang of kids from the year below was seated in the back. Chinedu knew the social code. As a senior he had the right to chase them off, but he didn't want to give them an excuse to start talking to him.

Chinedu flopped down on a weathered seat in the middle of the bus and planted his head against the window. He threw his bag atop the seat next to him to deter any potential inter-viewers. The sounds of Kanye West and Lupe Fiasco sheltered him from the escalating murmurs. Then, before he could close his eyes to truly get lost in his songs, MacKenzie stepped onto the bus. She found his eyes and waved innocuously. The only free seat left on the bus was beside him, so he knocked his bag unceremoniously to the floor.

MacKenzie sat down and at first looked straight ahead. They took turns turning to each other and repeatedly missed making eye contact again by split seconds. This was a dance that Chinedu could keep up for the entire bus ride. MacKenzie had the kind of looks that swallowed every other part of who she was. She was the captain of the volleyball team, the only team that had brought the school any kind of sustained athletic suc-cess. She was the star of the debate team and wrote frequently for the school newspaper as well. Regardless, MacKenzie was known as the "hot girl with ginger hair."

"How are you feeling about tomorrow?" she finally asked.

Chinedu tended to fumble his words around girls. He once tried probing his father about how to relate to girls and had received death stares. "Focus on your studies. Why do you want to gallivant with girls? Were you not home trained?"

"I think it's going to go well," Chinedu replied, but he could feel the strain in his voice. His mind had stopped to think that he could miss.

MacKenzie talked about the pressures of winning volleyball championships. She shook her head at how irrationally scared she always got. "I always feel like I'm going to throw up, and then the game starts and the fear slowly fades," she said. "At a certain point, you have to believe in and lean on all the preparation you've done." She was proud he had ignored Johnny Bombs and was excited to watch the free throws. Her support wasn't helpful.

Chinedu was pleased he had managed to chat with MacKenzie, as he trotted off the school bus and walked the rest of the way home. There were Hollywood movies that outlined how things could go: a dweeb who was counted out makes the shot and successfully becomes the unlikely hero and gets the girl. He thought about calling Vishal on the way home, but he knew he would be told to get real about MacKenzie. "Rightfully so," he thought, as he approached his house.

Chinedu rang the doorbell – he never carried the house key, and heard the rapid-fire clacking of high heels. His mother pulled the door open and flashed an especially wide grin. His father stood behind her with the whites of his teeth on full display. The smile and his being home early were both rare occurrences.

"We received a special invitation to come to your basketball game tomorrow," his mother squealed.

"They have a photo of you driving to the basket past some overgrown kid. Apparently you almost scored too," Papa Chinedu noted.

Chinedu's mother waved him inside, relieved him of his bag, and squeezed his shoulder before clacking away into the kitchen.

"Finally, you have your chance" his father boomed, and they sat together until dinner was ready.

His mother had prepared his favorite meal, an overflowing plate of fried rice, plantains, and three pieces of fried chicken. He was accustomed to getting one piece.

Papa Chinedu spoke at length about his day over the table. "Growing pains," he huffed as he recounted the trials of orienting his confused, new staff. He was a manager at a new telecommunications company. "These guys show up with their new degrees and wilt under the pressure," he moaned. He shot a look at Chinedu that was understood to mean "Don't be like them." Only one kind of wilt was welcome… Chamberlain.

They were not known to sit and socialize as a family for such long periods of time. Chinedu sensed they had reached their limit and cleaned the dishes before retreating to his room.

He opened his laptop only to see that Facebook had blown up. People kept tagging his name in their comments. He surfed the web to the best of his ability but kept drifting back to Facebook. He devoured all of the text about him even as it turned his stomach like a dryer. Just when he thought he had read it all, a new post popped up in his feed. He had been invited to a Facebook event called "Chinedu's Free Throws." He thought about working on his literature paper, but he convinced himself he was not that desperate for a reprieve. He went to bed but had trouble falling asleep, and when he finally did, he did not sleep for more than an hour at a time.

Chinedu barely ate breakfast the next morning. He figured he was less likely to throw up if his stomach was empty. He filled up on Gatorade and made his way to the gym. He had been excused from all classes before the noontime show. "Take the time to practice," the principal had written. With that, he was shooting air balls and running after missed shots alone on the basketball court. His stomach growled underneath his soaked shirt. He stopped shooting and sat at the free-throw line.

Three people visited him in turn, like the ghosts of Christmas. First came Principal Smith. He was stuffed into a yellow Honey Badgers shirt and matching cap. His scraggly beard had been trimmed and tamed. He strangled Chinedu's hand in what could only be classified as a man's handshake; he then explained what was at stake:

"We have asked the board to provide more support for our athletics program. Up until now, they have rejected the idea. If we win today though, I think they will have to come around. There may even be sponsorship opportunities on top of that too." He went on to rattle off benefits that included better training equipment, improved facilities, new jerseys, and access to player and coaching camps. "It would be a shame to lose out on all of that," he concluded. A wince was followed by a plastered smile before he turned and left. The conversation was efficient.

Then Coach burst in. His smile was over-the-top but genuine. He wore a Honey Badgers tracksuit and jacket instead of one of his tailored suits. He had run up and down in search of his player. Chinedu was still grappling with the realization that the growth of the athletics programs rested on his slim shoulders when Coach whooped, "Judith...I mean, my wife—oh, ex-wife—is coming to the game!" (Math Teacher Usher would have broken a muscle shaking his head, before exhaling, "I don't believe in sequels.")

Coach threw balls at Chinedu and yelled for him to shoot. He mimicked the whoops and hisses of the crowd. He waved his hands manically and made faces to distract him. He ran after and retrieved every errant ball. He offered advice on Chinedu's shooting mechanics and peppered him with encouragement. Coach, fully applying himself for the first time all season, was surprisingly good at his job.

Then his phone rang, and Chinedu watched his face glow like a jack-o'-lantern. Judith was on the other end of the line.

Mouthing an apology, Coach scampered off. Chinedu could hear him in the distance. His voice reached record highs in register. Chinedu was sure, even with his scant knowledge of women, that winning a high-school basketball tournament was not a dependable spark for fixing a broken relationship.

If he could have dictated events, MacKenzie would have been the third person to walk into the gym. She would tell him how to ignore the grown-man problems that had been shoveled onto him. She would dab away his case of nerves and restore his belief.

Instead, Johnny Bombs emerged from the locker room. He was in full playing uniform, adorned with kneepads, elbow pads, and finger pads. Johnny scooped up the ball and launched it from the three-point line. The ball tickled the inside of the net on the way through. Swish.

"That's what would've happened yesterday," he snapped. Johnny fetched the ball again, stood at the free-throw line, and threw the ball up. Swish. "You forgot your place," he spat. Johnny brushed stray strands of hair behind his ear while staring his new nemesis down.

The words "your place" cannoned through Chinedu's head. If he jumped, he could probably retaliate with a head butt to the nose.

"We still have a chance though," Johnny continued. "Be a man, and say that you slipped in the locker-room shower. Pretend that you twisted your ankle or rolled your wrist. Then I'll step in for you and shoot the free throws."

"The other team gets to pick the replacement," Chinedu retorted.

"Their coach is a family friend. I'm sure he will be a gentleman about it," Johnny countered, "and everyone will hate you if you choose to be stubborn."

With that, the gauntlet had been thrown down. Chinedu could shoot the free throws and risk everyone's ire or defer and earn the permanent disdain of his father. His high-school life was pitted against his family life.

"You need to be in class, John," Coach interjected.

Johnny Bombs made to say something, nixed the idea, and mouthed, "I'll be back," on his way out.

Coach and Chinedu practiced for another half hour before Coach suggested that his player take a breather.

Chinedu relaxed the best way he knew how, in a plastic chair, wolfing down shawarmas from Mr. Arvind. In a less complicated time, back when Chinedu and his teammates were pimple-faced ninth graders, they played basketball on the outdoor courts during recess until their school polos became drenched with sweat. People from the losing team had to hop the fence to get everyone shawarmas. They sat around and recounted who made the most shots. The ritual faded when they all got older because the girls they had crushes on grew less tolerant about sitting next to sweaty, panting boys.

Mr. Arvind tried to contain himself. He could see the pressure in Chinedu's face, suddenly aged and wrinkled like papyrus. He glanced furtively at his lone customer and finally said, "Good luck, bro. This time it is on the house." Chinedu squirmed, imagining the awkwardness of his next visit to Mr. Arvind's if he missed.

Chinedu ate four more shawarmas, not to take advantage of his fleeting celebrity, but to crowd out the butterflies in his stomach. He climbed back over the fence and headed back to the gym.

The locker room was littered with abandoned towels, shorts, and unpaired socks. The air had a sticky, sweaty flavor. The white walls were so heavily covered with sports paraphernalia that a graffiti artist would have to pack up and go elsewhere. Chinedu spent his last moments cowed on one of the benches. He scrunched his eyes, clasped his hands, and broke out into prayer, a sight his mother would have appreciated since he often forgot to do so.

When he opened his eyes, he felt as if he were returning from another place; Johnny Bombs was there to welcome him back, still dressed in full uniform.

"Remember what to say," he barked.

———

The gym was transformed. Pictures of Honey Badgers clung to every wall. Plastic chairs, similar to the ones at Mr. Arvind's, surrounded the court to seat all of the extra spectators. Principal Smith was armed and ready to go with a megaphone up in the rafters. He roused everyone he glimpsed stepping into the gym. Coach sat on the bench with the rest of the team in their tracksuits. Johnny Bombs began to tell them all about how Chinedu had rolled his ankle, but Coach looked past him, scanning the growing crowd for Judy.

Johnny looked up into the crowd at the Chinedu posters, which should have been Johnny Bomb posters. There was a blow-up photo hanging from one of the railings of Chinedu making a layup. Above all the other voices, MacKenzie yelled, "Chinedu!"

The other team sat on their bench in uniform too, in case the free throws were split. Johnny was making his way to tell them about how he was to replace Chinedu as the shooter when everyone in the gym stood up in unison. The volume was cranked up to eleven. When Johnny looked back, Chinedu was standing on the court.

A tear fell down Johnny's cheek in mourning at the passing of the peak of his life. He was a big fish in a small pond with no shot at legitimate college basketball. School was a slog that was only going to get worse, so he was far from excited about the next frontier. He saw himself treading water in anonymity from then on.

Chinedu looked as if he were about to throw up, like the shawarmas had been a bad idea, and Johnny felt the same way. At the sight of him, the referee blew the whistle, walked past Johnny, and gave Chinedu the game ball.

Chinedu stared, in succession, back at Johnny Bombs, into the lenses of the courtside cameras, at the game ball, and at the rim with its new net on. He heard his heart beat, heard Principal Smith on the megaphone, heard Coach, heard MacKenzie and an ensemble of alien voices. He didn't hear his father. He heard the referee's whistle again, and then there was nothing else to hear. He was a speck drifting alone in the cosmos.

One bounce, bend your knees, three bounces, exhale, pause…

He watched the basketball rise and fall and splash. Nothing but net. The gymnasium itself gasped.

"One shot to rule them all," he whispered to himself. He almost laughed at the corniness of the remark. The referee passed the ball back to him, but it rocketed through Chinedu's hands and cannoned off his chest because his attention had been drawn elsewhere. He finally saw Papa Chinedu up in the rafters, with his mother beside him. His father gave him a head nod.

Chinedu was surprised he did not feel more excited. To win the game in front of his father was a once-in-a-lifetime chance, but he found that his motives were more selfish. He was not chomping at the bit to get Principal Smith his sponsorship money or to make Coach look impressive in front of his ex-wife or to win MacKenzie's adoration. He didn't want to show up Johnny Bombs for sulking behind him. The final shot was for him and by him, like FUBU. He had worked hard for it, and quite frankly, in the moment, he didn't need any more motivation.

He knew he could forgive himself for missing, too, whether or not everyone else could. People who had not cared about basketball two days ago and would not two days on now leaned in as if their mortgages depended on it.

So once again: one bounce, bend your knees, three bounces, exhale, pause…

Then, watch them rush the court.

Summer 2013

2

Switching Lanes

A RAP ON the door jarred Augustine Okoroji awake. He let out a string of swear words but remained cocooned in bed. A breakfast tray was slid into his confines, and Augustine engaged it in a staring contest until his cavernous stomach gave in. He slipped out of bed, clawed the tray toward him, but could only pick morosely at the careless mishmash of oatmeal and baked beans. He did not follow Oliver Twist's example. His once plump cheeks had hollowed out, and he had been forced to punch extra holes into his belt. Augustine munched the crackers and scattered the rest of the food around his plate like an adolescent looking to deceive his mother. He missed waking up to *akamu*, *akara*, and a mug of hot Ovaltine, all garnished with a side of love from his doting wife, Nkechi.

Augustine's room was little more than an empty vessel with four gray walls and two small, mocking windows. There was little to suggest that anyone had lived there for two months except for the lump that was there, shifting listlessly in bed. His family had visited regularly during the first month of his stint, but he'd done little to engage in amicable conversations, volleying away their pleasantries. His daughter, Nnenna, begged with crinkled brow that he eat his meals and shave his silver, burgeoning wizard's beard.

"Nonsense," he often clucked.

He sank lower in his seat with each subsequent visit. If he kept it up, in time only his spiraling Afro would be above the table. Augustine only spoke at length to demand that they work on getting him released. He was seventy-five years old, ornery, and lonely. There were brief moments in which, sitting across from them, his eyes threatened to leak. Then, he blinked furiously and shook his head, casting any signs of sadness as a mirage.

"I used to live in a three-story house that I built myself. I shouldn't be here," he declared.

His grandson honored their bond, forged over episodes of *Top Gear*, by nodding repeatedly at such statements. Augustine spoke at length about the different cars he had driven in Nigeria, and painted a life that his young namesake, whose name had been filed down to Austin, hoped to inherit.

Austin's father, a tired insurance agent, scrunched his face whenever Austin waddled over and pitched a desire to live in

Nigeria. His grandfather Augustine was like no other adult in Austin's life. Augustine carried himself in a manner that merited having a parasol in every drink. His voice had a richer bass, his clothes were more vibrant, and his rough hands felt like they had history etched in them. The family ate Mexican American fusions at the table while Nnenna delivered Nigerian cuisine to her father on a tray in front of the television. But soon Augustine had found a second wind and lived in a bubble that no one else had access to. Austin was ten years old, but if he were a teenager, he would have simply called his grandfather a "boss."

"I want granddad to come home."

"That's my protégé," Augustine cackled.

"It is not like you are in jail," Nnenna interjected. She shook her head slowly. Every visit aged her.

"Easy for you to say," her father grunted back. He kept a painted smile on his face for his grandson's sake, but he felt a fog descending over him again. He always made sure to leave the table in the courtyard before he detonated. He excused himself and hurried away without looking back. His black-and-gold cane dragged in the grass, struggling to keep up. The cane was one of the few things he had ever taken out of the suitcase under his bed upon arriving at the New Day Home for the Elderly. Augustine Okoroji had packed and unpacked as if he was only going to be gone for a matter of days. He had misjudged his daughter's resolve.

Nnenna Torres felt her heart break each time her old man re-treated. She saw his anguish in the way his gaze scooted too quickly from one face to another. In his heyday managing car dealerships in Nigeria, his eyes had contained an infectious passion that helped him flood streets with Peugeot 505s. Before he set tongues wagging at the prospect of hopping into new cars, he had at times, growing up, debated his way out of his parents' punishments. His charisma had only abandoned him twice: when he met Jose Torres and the moment he was consigned to the retirement home. Of late, he fumbled his words as if an NFL linebacker had tackled him out of his black leather loafers.

Jose Torres was the last family member to visit Augustine, and he did so all by himself. Austin asked to come along and wailed at being robbed of a visit. Jose had many things to say, but his voice was hoarse because he spent more time shouting than talking in any kind of normal tone.

When Nnenna had first told Jose that his father-in-law was coming from Nigeria to live with them, he'd shouted. When he had to spend his Saturday afternoon looking for semolina for Augustine's dinner, he shouted. When his four children tried to eat on their laps in front of the television, he shouted. When Nnenna would not agree to send Augustine to a retirement home, he shouted. And when Nnenna argued that they should consider letting him come back home, he shouted the most.

Jose and Nnenna had a son, a daughter, and twin girls. Augustine, to Jose, was the imported fifth child who did not care for him.

Augustine had written Jose off from the beginning for failing to ask for his daughter's hand in marriage. The villainy was compounded when there was no traditional Nigerian wedding. Jose did not call Augustine "Dee" or "Sir" or "Oga," as was customary, either. In fact, Jose had tried to christen Augustine as "Gus."

His grandchildren did not know a word of Igbo but spoke decent Spanish. They didn't know the Nigerian national anthem but belted out "The Star-Spangled Banner."

Nnenna had played peacemaker between the two men's passive-aggressiveness toward each other without success. She once thought that the two men would bond over their interest in sales. Selling cars and selling insurance are two different things though.

At the retirement home's courtyard on that last visit, Jose never lifted his eyes from the table while explaining that for the good of everyone involved, the family was taking a break from seeing Augustine. He felt himself flinch, but no retort came his way. Finally, his voice could rest.

While Jose was at the retirement home on this last visit, Nnenna fiddled with her car keys at home and wrestled with the idea of driving out to talk to her father herself. She pictured her father eating her husband alive, but her palms became clammy thinking about a showdown of her own. There was an invisible barrier between her father and her that was seldom scaled. She often worried about whether he wished for a son instead of (or at least in addition to) her. If not, maybe he blamed her for her tardy arrival into the world.

Augustine and Nkechi had been married for ten years before Nnenna was born. The couple had first gotten to work on a baby the moment the door closed behind the last of their wedding guests.

"He loves you, but our men don't show it too well," her mother often said in comfort.

In the sixties and well before, right up to the seventies, and eighties, a man who supported a large family commanded significant respect in Nigeria. This was arguably an artifact of a bygone era, but back in Nigeria, younger Augustine saw gaping chasms when he looked at the empty spaces that engulfed their only child in the backseat of their car. He had no problems though making the utmost investments in his daughter. In 1990, he sent her off to the United States for college. Nnenna's mother stressed what to do and not to do, made her promise to call at least twice a week, and unloaded reams of advice before her face started streaming. Augustine nodded at her and pointed toward the gate. He called a couple of times a semester. Each time they spoke, her accent sounded a little different, and words he did not quite understand steadily invaded their short conversations. The invisible barrier stood tall.

In truth, Augustine missed his daughter dearly. He rattled on about how well she was doing as an economics and prelaw student overseas. The same friends who whispered about his small family let out "oohs" and "ahs" and repeatedly cheered "Praise the Lord" at all of the good news about Nnenna. He grinned to himself from ear to ear but made fun of Nkechi for her incessant phone calls and gratuitous displays of affection. The couple would have been best served talking to each other about how their empty nest had affected each of them, but they said little and sputtered on. Augustine and Nkechi had lived together for ten years after all before Nnenna was born. Augustine never thought he would end up living completely alone though. He ate too heartily, drank too much, and spoiled himself with too many "just this once" cigarettes to outlive his wife. Nkechi played her part by jogging regularly, eating salads, and frowning at the mention of drinking alcohol.

Life did not comply. When Nkechi turned sixty, she fell ill and died quicker than Augustine could process. Her death left Augustine alone in the three-story house he had built a quarter century before. The house had always been oversized, devised for a large family. Then it took on a truly vacuous personality with only one tenant. He retired, blaming work for distracting him from noticing the depth of his wife's ailments. He walked through the house as if he had been dropped in the wilderness. Inflicted with rust, he slowly reacquainted himself with the concept of chores. He cooked, cleaned, did laundry, and took out the trash all for the first time in over forty years. Nnenna called as often as her mother had called her back when she was in college. Augustine's answers were curt, maintaining that he was doing fine. Just when she thought he was in fact doing fine, unknown numbers from extended family members she struggled to remember hijacked her phone.

"He calls to ask whether I know where the extra bedsheets are kept. How would I know that?" one family member groaned.

"We invite him to come and visit, and he says that he is busy, but I know that he is lying," another lamented.

When her phone finally lay still, catching its breath, she decided her father needed to come to America to be with the rest of his loved ones.

Augustine was skeptical about the proposed arrangement. He was broken but determined to mask it. He convinced himself that his daughter and grandchildren needed him, which was the only way to get him to travel to a new, mystical land.

The eventual meeting with Jose painted over the pictures in his head. His family didn't need him. They didn't want him. His son-in-law basked in the ease and success of his encounter but soon found new reasons to strain his voice. When clients sheepishly said no to his health, home, and life insurance bundles, he shouted. When Nnenna asked him to do more at home because she was swamped with cases, he shouted. When it became clear they were moving in opposite directions in their careers, he shouted. The coup de grace: when he realized he was still shouting, he shouted.

Austin Torres wanted to shout too because he missed his grandfather. The last visit stuck in his head because it was the last time they had all gone out as a family. Austin felt as if the adults were hiding from him. They trooped in and out like windup dolls. Nnenna spent more time buried in legal cases while Jose was determined to match her stride. Austin endured his ten-year-old battles in silence. He was raised by cameo appearances.

Jose would have told his son Austin to deal with his problems much differently if he had been aware of them. Part of Austin already knew what he was supposed to do, and his fist realized he had chosen poorly the moment he punched Charlie Ross in the face. His knuckle felt like it had been run into a brick wall, but Charlie's nose started running. All Austin wanted to do was chat about cars and play soccer in recess. He stared into Charlie's reddened, raging face and waited for him to lurch. Charlie was the tallest, beefiest kid in grade five. Calling him "beefy" instead of "fat" was per his orders. He ate a lot of people's lunches as any good bully should, but it was his ability to taunt that unnerved Austin the most.

"Want to sneak stuff out of Ahmed's? No? Really? See, I knew you were yellow. You are yellower than a submarine. You don't get it? Well, that's because you are still a baby!" A horde of kids circled them like spectators at the coliseum. Charlie blinked, rubbed his bloody nose, and swore. Austin kept his fists up. The fight ended there because Charlie fell into a shock that can come from being hit for the first time. As furious as he was, he did not want the event to happen again. That Austin was soon tugged away by a gruff pair of hands allowed him to save face.

Mr. Drummond gave his report to Principal Stern and left Austin alone in the sterile office. The principal called his mother, but she was in court arguing a case—unavailable. His father was at an insurance conference—unavailable. The principal tried to talk to the boy before her, but he seemed to have had an out-of-body experience. She was dealing with the Hulk back as Bruce Banner.

"Could you call my grandfather please?" he whispered.

Principal Stern sat atop her desk and stared at the increasingly meek child before her. Heather Smith, a caretaker at the home, answered the call for Augustine but missed him by a matter of minutes. As she huffed her way up and down the retirement home, she remembered the days when she could bet her pension on finding Augustine holed up in his fortress of solitude. Austin's principal remained on hold, listening to jazz music. Heather finally found Augustine in the basement with Titus and Sue.

Titus was eighty-three years old but taunted time with his chiseled body. He was how Sylvester Stallone could only wish to age, but he might have offered his skin as a sacrifice because it was extraordinarily leathery. Augustine initially wondered whether he was from Senegal but found out that he'd been born and raised in Brooklyn. He was bald under his bucket hat and was rich behind his lips. The two men met when

Titus plopped down at Augustine's table to tell a moribund Augustine, "These young cats don't understand."

Augustine learned that he was well known throughout the home. Bets had been placed on how long it would take for him to start a conversation, to come to the cafeteria, and to erupt into an open display of insanity.

"I wish that us getting you to join our band was one of the bets," Titus lamented. Sue laughed sonorously. She was eighty-three years old as well. Her hair was a long, wavy gray and worthy of being featured in Pantene commercials. She played the drums and usually set up to Titus's right. She conceded the spot to Augustine so that the new crooner and the musical savant could bond. Titus was deaf in his left ear. Titus could play more instruments than Augustine knew about. "You want Fela?" he often teased.

When Heather tracked Augustine down, Sue was guiding Augustine through the singing of Augustana's "Boston." Sue was from Boston. Heather interrupted Augustana to give Augustine the handset to speak to Austin's principal. Ten minutes later, Heather had her head in her hands in the backseat of her car.

"I know cars," Augustine assured her. He showed her a Nigerian driver's license with a picture from years ago. There was a lump in her throat that would have been larger had she let them go without her.

Augustine quickly felt as if he were trying to control an untamed animal. In the years gone by, cars had become difficult to maneuver. Did they not make them like they used to? Gently at first, and then with resounding authority, Heather took back the reins. Being in her midtwenties, she found it difficult to command the elderly people she worked with. She wanted to be a friend and confidant, not an overseer or superintendent.

"Things change," Sue said.

"Yes, they do," Augustine replied.

The car left him dumbfounded. It was as if the vehicle had forgotten they'd been star-crossed lovers.

Heather normally drove carefree. She listened to NPR in the morning and loudly played Top 40 radio on the way back from work. Augustine noticed that her fuel and oil levels were begging for attention. He let it go, out of respect for his defeat.

The school hallways were deserted and cloaked in silence when they arrived. Augustine, Heather, and Titus walked past windows with kids sitting quietly: some, bored; others, clearly in faraway lands. They witnessed the flying of spitballs and the sliding of notes. Then, a large wooden door with the words "Principal Stern" leaped at them. Augustine walked in alone, which was for the best because Principal Stern's office would have become claustrophobic if it had needed to accommodate six people. Austin looked up at his grandfather and tried to suppress a smile. Principle Stern launched into Austin's charges firmly but politely. She fought the urge to apologize to the man before him for forcing him to come to the school. Augustine listened calmly. He was permitted to take his grandson home, a wish he had harbored for himself.

The namesakes hugged once they got out to the car. Austin clutched at his grandfather's shirt, and the frowns melted all around. Austin sat between Titus and Augustine on the way home, and all manner of thought tumbled out of him. He told them about the highs and lows of playing soccer, how annoying but sweet but oh so annoying a girl called Angela in his class was, how excited he was about Musa's birthday party, how he wanted to be a race-car driver and an astronaut. He gave a commentary about how bullying was wrong but that he was ever so sorry. All the while, Titus and Augustine listened and exchanged grins over his head.

Augustine flirted with the idea of heading to the closet pool, when his daughter's house came into view.

"You are home free!" Titus whooped as they pulled up.

"I will be back," Augustine assured.

"No, I will beg mum to let you stay," Austin moaned. "She will come around."

"Things change," Augustine replied.

A black Camry pulled up behind them, and both Nnenna and Jose peeled out and scurried toward them. They had stumbled onto the messages left by the school because Jose had become intensely bored at his insurance conference. He became distracted by his phone and listened to his voicemail, which launched a chain of events that included driving to see, interrupt, and pick up Nnenna. A baffled assistant remained in court in her stead.

Austin was relieved to see that all of the adults were back. None of them knew how to soothe their injured relationship, but the invisible barriers were going to come down.

Things change.

Summer 2013

3

Switching Lanes Faster

B EING HOME ALONE made Austin king of the castle, but he was looking to abscond from atop his throne. He sat on a stool in the kitchen, legs swaying, as he sipped a carton of apple juice. The clock on the wall told the same story whenever he glared up at it. Linus was late.

Austin began to fidget when the Jeep Wrangler finally pulled up. He bounded outside, and blotches of rain tagged him until he made it to the passenger seat of a car his mother forbade him from riding in. Linus sat slouched with one hand on the wheel and a smirk plastered on his face. He waved his other arm in a halfhearted attempt to rid the Wrangler of its cigarette smell.

"You look spiffy," he chuckled.

Austin shrugged. He felt like an overqualified clothes hanger in his white collared shirt, khaki trousers, and polished pair of dark brown loafers. He usually had to be coerced into wrapping himself in his Sunday best. His grandfather always appreciated when he dressed up though, so he surrendered to the heavily starched garments.

"I am taking Tyler to laser tag. Are you sure you don't want to come along instead?" Linus asked. "Hanging out with the TiTy boys is always a good time—especially on a day off."

Austin shook his head though. Every day was a day off for Linus. "I need to see my grandpa," he insisted.

So the Wrangler ceded to his will and sputtered into life.

Despite the months that had passed between visits, Austin knew every turn to the retirement home. Defying suspicion, Linus proved to be a responsible driver. With a pierced eyebrow, tattooed arms, and a standing claim that he was an artist, parents employed him as a cautionary tale before even talking to him. All Austin knew was that some of Linus's paintings would look good in the house.

Linus was built for road trips, especially as far as Austin was concerned. As a nineteen-year-old, he had seen so much more of the world, and unlike the adults, he was willing to share its secrets. He came armed with stories about falling in love, being chased out of his girlfriend's house by her father, and how it felt to get his heart broken. He confided that his first tattoo had hurt so much it had almost scared him off from getting another one ever again. He had hidden the tattoo under long-sleeve shirts for close to three months. His eyes lit up when he talked about the days he drove the Wrangler with no map and no planned destination. He left whether to turn left, right, or go straight to his gut.

"I go somewhere alien to me, sit on the hood of the car, and draw until the sun goes down. Then I go home. I always come back home."

There were times when Linus's stream of consciousness flowed so freely that Austin felt like he had rented space in his mind. He paused when the retirement home came into view.

"Here, yeah?"

"Yeah."

The faithful driver ruffled his appreciative passenger's budding Afro. "Wow, it is almost as big as mine now. I don't like the competition," he laughed. His fingers served as pistols while he mimicked the sound of lasers.

<hr>

Evelyn, a receptionist at the home, was wrapping up a conversation when she saw Austin and gestured that he hurry over out of the rain. She wore a green raincoat and matching Wellingtons. Austin was sat down in the courtyard, which was where all of their family visits occurred. "It is so nice that your parents were able to drop you off to see Mr. Okoroji," Evelyn chirped. "I was getting worried that no one was going to visit anymore!" She smelled like baked goods and revealed her secret as she offered him a cupcake. She then promised to find his grandfather, squelching away in the green boots.

The courtyard was covered with wooden picnic tables. Well-trimmed hedges surrounded the area, and various flowerbeds took up pockets of space as well. Some of the residents enjoyed tending to the plants, but with the rain pelting, none of them were in sight. Neither were the men who usually huddled together, engrossed in card games and animated discussions about news and politics and all the girls they'd known when they were younger. Austin's eyes gravitated toward an elderly lady who was beaming so much her wrinkles seemed to fade with each second. She was seated with a boy and a girl who were probably her grandchildren. They were the only other people out in the courtyard, shielded as he was by an umbrella that poked through and covered the picnic tables.

Austin saw Evelyn again. He looked beyond her to see whether his grandfather was strolling just behind with his black-and-gold cane. She wore a look that said otherwise. Her once immaculate brown bun looked ruffled.

"I checked his room, but he was not there. Can you sit tight? Would you like another cupcake?" Austin longed for another cupcake, but he didn't want to take advantage of her kindness. This decision would please his mother, and it was the least he could do after driving to the retirement home in Linus's car, without her consent. His taste buds protested.

———⚬⚬⚬———

Evelyn remembered a time when one could bet one's pension that Augustine Okoroji would be found nowhere else but in his room. Each morning, a knock on the door stirred him awake. The half-eaten meals were the only things that left the room. Soon, Evelyn was being asked what the over and under should be on Mr. Okoroji ever coming out.

The one stipulation was that leaving the room to see visitors did not count. The bet did come to an end after Alvaro Torres came to see Augustine.

Austin stuck his hand out from under the table's umbrella. Raindrops pecked his palm every quarter of a minute or so. The blue of the sky was peeking through the clouds. Evelyn returned to find him staring upward. She shook her head repeatedly, and her hair splayed because she had undone her bun completely.

"Your grandpa seems to be busy right now," she said. She could not contain the strain in her voice. "I will drive you home and talk briefly to your parents." Austin looked at his neon watch and saw that time had been munched away. They could probably beat them home but not by much. He got to his feet, but his heart raced as they stepped away from the courtyard. He knew that Evelyn was, at the very least, bending the truth. The reception smelled like a Febreze demonstration. Evelyn had found herself a substitute. Austin's eyes welled up with each step toward the parking lot. Where was Grandpa Augustine?

Evelyn steered him toward her 2004 Camry, with one arm placed on his quivering shoulder. Austin bit his lip, kicked at the asphalt, and made no move to get in through the passenger-side door that she opened.

"Where is my grandpa?" he finally bellowed.

—◆—

Evelyn placed her hand on her head while her lower lip wobbled. She had gone to the cafeteria where jazz music was softly threaded through the speakers. The residents were served lunch and dinner meals from personalized, preapproved lists of food. At the time, a group of men and women were playing bingo. She checked the workout room where a couple of women walked side by side on a treadmill, deep in conversation. Staff members watched in silence on the edge of their seats. The workout room was a neglected, expansive space. Evelyn even peeked into the music room where Augustine sang from time to time with a postshowdown friend called Titus. She found Titus there playing guitar by himself. The instrument looked small in his muscled arms, but he held it delicately. He smiled, flashing a gold tooth, and said he was making up the melodies as he went.

Austin, while often a recipient of the distinction himself, was not going to give an A for effort. Evelyn fanned at her face although it was not hot outside. She would have to report Augustine's disappearance immediately. Her Wellingtons squeaked as she made her way back inside.

But then, she was forced to stop. Two men stood together clothed in blue overalls and smatterings of grease. The younger man was wide-eyed, nodding so fervently that blond tresses swayed in front of his eyes like window wipers. The older man—the much older man—sported a hedge of gray beard that hung at the young man's eye level. Surprisingly, his hair was close-cropped. The old man stood slightly hunched and wiped his hands with a small towel. The old man held Evelyn's gaze, and with that, she bathed in a sense of relief with a hand placed against her heart.

Austin saw the old man too.

"Grandpa Augustine!" he squealed.

"My protégé!" he cheered.

Austin wrapped his arms around the original. He looked like he had been eating more. "This is perfect timing. Do you know why?" Austin shook his head, so Augustine stepped back to fully expose a lemon-colored 1980 Fiat Spider. The black top to the convertible was dropped. "The owner of this home wants to pass this car along to his son here, but he needed help fixing it. My friend Titus recommended me, and here we are." He gave a mock bow before ruffling Austin's Afro.

"Best of all, he said I can drive it out if I fix it, and I believe it will purr when I fire it up."

"Is that safe?" Evelyn chimed in from a few steps away.

"I was a mechanic and a car dealer. Even at this age, this is right up my alley, Mrs. Chipman," he said. He flashed an American driver's license and added, "Ryan will look out for me and drive me back." With that, Augustine ferried Ryan and Austin into the revitalized car. He fished his phone out of his overalls and called his daughter. He barely used it, but Titus insisted he keep it on to receive his hilarious messages—and also, in case the family called. Augustine left a voice message. Nnenna was probably stuck in an important meeting. He said, "I love you," at the end, but the words flopped out like a fish out of water because he was not fine-tuned to say them.

Young and youngest sat excitedly in the car, their eyes round like moons. Ryan had kindly fumbled into the back of the Spider. Augustine gave Evelyn a confident wave and slid into the car himself. The engine did not purr. The engine hacked and wheezed like the most infected of men, but it found its lungs after a nervous minute. The Spider felt like an untamed beast of a whole other nature at first, but he soon gained its obedience.

"I still wish you could come home. Please keep trying," Austin sighed.

"Sometimes you have to eat enchiladas instead of *eba*," Augustine chuckled. His grandson stared blankly.

"Well, OK. When I lost your grandmother…wow…I missed her so very much. I miss her every day. Our house became an oversized shell. I called your aunties to find out where the extra bedsheets were kept. As if they would know? Kai, I was lost. I am still lost. I needed to come to America to be with my family, to be with you. This retirement-home stuff is not how we do things back home. I know. Your Momsi though is pushing herself so hard at her law firm. Your father is doing the same. I am seventy-five now, but I can still support all of you in my own way." He looked outside the windows at unfamiliar streets. "I am not sure where we are by the way. We might be on an adventure."

"That is fine," Austin replied. "Sometimes you have to go somewhere with no map and no planned destination. Somewhere alien to you. Before sunset."

"This whole country is still alien to me."

"Then we better get going, Grandpa! That just means there is so much to see."

September 15, 2013

4

Musketeers

I HAVE HEARD a lot of theories about manhood that I know are way off. So, I have conducted my own research on the matter and now realize that a clear answer might elude me forever. I first felt manly after rallying against the sullying of Spiderman.

Before I say anything else, it is important to acknowledge that before things went sour with *Spiderman 3*, watching the Spiderman movies was a childhood highlight. I saw the first Tobey Maguire film on a projector in the chapel of the place then dubbed the "Local Jail for Children." My friends and I pooled together our favorite moments from the film and stored them like treasure troves in our collective memories. We would keep them in reserve for the next time we were holed up and bored in class.

One day, we were quickly surrounded in the chapel area by The Herd once we got back to the dormitories. This towering gang of seven snickered over us mischievously, basking in snagging their prey. The Herd herded us into the chapel and ordered us to place both the palms of our hands and the soles of our feet against the ceiling in honor of Spiderman. I wish I could trace back where the elixir of courage came from, but after defiantly watching feats of heroism from a chapel pew, I had to separate myself from the sight of kids tumbling off of each other's backs. I tore away with my hands jammed in my pockets as the room turned into a convention for contortionists.

No one came after me. I later found out it was because The Herd figured that I suffered from temporary, correctable insanity. My best friend, Chiddy, sat by my bed the next day with a tumbling mountain of uniforms. Redemption lay in ironing them for The Herd. Every day we wore white shirts, navy-blue trousers, white socks, and brown loafers to class. The school generously gave us our regular sports attire and clothes for leisure too. I still mourn the loss of my lucky Manchester United jersey, seized as contraband and lost forever. Such was life at the Local Jail for Children.

I thought about punting away the inherited mound of garments. I saw the kids that dragged their feet, slouched through the hallways, and stared glumly at the ground as they trudged up and down campus. Those kids would find a can of starch and scoop the clothes up with defeat etched onto their faces. I liked my newfound cavalier attitude and wanted to preserve the privilege of keeping my chin in the air. Holes get burned in shirts quicker than I imagined. A skinny twelve-year-old who gets clubbed by an angry eighteen-year-old drops quicker than I imagined as well. There is also the fact that getting punched hurts. Your eyes bathe in acid. Your lip trembles as if your face is embroiled in a mild earthquake. Your legs turn to spaghetti, ignoring the barks of your brain to get up.

The young witnesses were astounded. While I tried not to die inside and out, a discovery had been made. Saying no was an option. Once my ineffectual feet got me through the door, I became the hero of the downtrodden. One could say that the door to manhood rocked open. No great arbitrator ticked a box though and said, "All right, sir, you have shown us your credentials. You are now a man. As you were." The beady preteen eyes that clung to me only brought pressure.

I walked around with an overdose of pep in my step. I was applying for my SAG card though because my nerves lay in tatters. Had I paid the full penalty? I was one bad rumor away from swapping a plate of baked beans for hideout space under Tiny Tony's bed. I knew of kids who had successfully sought refuge under there before. Dust coated their arms and scrambled up their nostrils, but they felt secure even though Tony treated the underside of his bed like extra closet space.

Tony stood at five feet six inches, but he was built like a house and had a dash of crazy in him. He never reneged on a deal and was weirdly fond of baked beans. I lay under my own bed to test whether I could grow accustomed to such a life-style choice. I stared at the haphazard wire patterns that supported my mattress and thought about whether it was best to just apologize. The problem was that while everyone preached diplomacy, no one thought much highly of it. The shirt burner was much cooler.

I was pulled out of my quagmire by the rapid-fire snap of my room's screen door. I was so consumed in thought that I did not hear the morning bell. The eleven boys I shared the room with had just emptied out to joust for hot water. Six beds lay on opposite sides of the room. On the other walls rested a conjoined set of wardrobes. Our belongings gobbled most of the floor space. Knowing that I would have to start my morning off with a cold shower, I went to find Chiddy. Chiddy lived with Tony, too, so there was the added prospect of discussing protection services with him.

Whenever it felt like things had blown over, I'd get a sickening stare from someone in The Herd or hear the entrails of a conversation that I knew in my gut was about me. I was troubled, but I discovered that morning that there were people in greater distress than I was. My buddy Chiddy lay coiled in a heap on his bed. His sobbing was like the sound the cows made before getting killed by the kitchen staff. Chiddy blubbered about it being the worst birthday ever and dropped two limp notes into my hands. The first note was from his mother. She was a nice woman, but she had probably set him up to fail by pampering him so much. An example of this was the care package she sent him on his birthday. She mailed off enough confectionaries to keep dentists in the area employed for years; I had to rein in my saliva. Chiddy's mother had also gotten him new soccer shoes, some of his favorite comics, and a gold watch because he was "all grown up." Chiddy received none of these things because the package had been raided. All that was left was a torn sheet of graph paper that read, "Thanks for the treats, biznitch."

I was too used to Chiddy crying. During the weekends, we all had to do morning jogs that lasted so long they felt like East African running camps. In a matter of minutes, Chiddy could be found wheezing, doubled over. At times our jogging instructor stopped us and blew a whistle in his face. Boys in The Herd often fell back to encourage him with jabs to the stomach or ran backward alongside him for a good minute. Chiddy manufactured sick notes to skip the morning torture, so The Herd ate his food and crowed that they were dedicated to helping him lose weight. He was doomed. He was the boy who'd abandoned hot Joanna, his crush, because their long walks were making him late to the cafeteria. I didn't even bat an eye when he told me about ditching her. We all loved food. Food comforted your innards and restored your faith in the world amid the troubles that awaited you everywhere else on campus. While I was confined to boarding school, I would take a loaf of bread over a hundred dollars. That kind of money can't buy me headphones good enough to drown out the sound of a crying stomach. Chiddy might have kept his crying to an acceptable level on any other day, but instead the dam burst.

"I know who took my stuff," Chiddy finally murmured. He didn't have to debrief me on who the guys were. I was scared that the same group would dislodge my head from my shoulders.

"OK, what are you going to do about it?" I asked with immediate regret. The question was cruel because we both knew the answer. Chiddy was not going to do anything—again.

We stared awkwardly at and around each other. I opened my mouth to speak a couple of times, but each attempt ended up being a false start. Tiny Tony sat cross-legged on his bed with a pen and moleskin journal in hand until he could no longer tolerate the unfolding scene. He commanded respect even though he wore white pajamas in a world where everyone slept in boxers. He took off his reading glasses, carefully placed his retainer in a small plastic case, and gave us the mandate of our lives:

"Your friend here cries ugly," he began.

I nodded profusely. He smelled like talcum powder.

"Do you know the Three Musketeers? You need to make like the musketeers: all for one and one for all. OK?" he growled.

We nodded.

"Good. Now get out of my room and go and act like men," he charged.

Chiddy had never heard Tony speak for so long in one go before. We scampered off without delay, shook like flags in the wind from our cold showers, and most importantly, we talked ourselves into starting a revolution.

⚒

Tony might have been a hypnotist or primed for a career in politics. Chiddy alleged that his biceps were just so large that

— 50 —

we had no choice but to do as he said. Either way, we made like the musketeers. I marveled at the mass of people who sat with us on the patchy, beaten-down grass of the junior soccer field. The older boys turned their noses up at the sickly, yellowing field, so it was a great place to gather. In turn, we never stepped onto the well-trimmed, fervently watered, lush varsity field. Our goal posts had no nets, so when we scored, we trekked long distances, often into the bushes, to retrieve the ball.

"Be more delicate when you score!"

"Shut your mouth, loser, and get the ball!"

We dreamed of sliding indulgently over the turf after scoring goals, but all that awaited us were smarting, cut-up knees. The teachers repeated the fallacy that the varsity field was for all of us, and we nodded absently.

Getting kids there to join us in action was surprisingly easy. The revolution was not too complicated an idea. Boarding school sucked because everyone had a tale of woe to settle. My cult status as "The Shirt Burner" also gave me the clout to lead this consortium of sufferers.

"Should we bring weapons?" a voice yelped. The suggestion caromed against my ears like a spitball in class. I let the query hang in the air as long as I could. I had decided that a nonviolent show of unity was best, but another resounding voice bellowed, "Yes! We are not pansies." The crowd roared in approval, and I did not want to lose them so quickly, so I said nothing. I had gathered twenty or so of the most bloodthirsty boys around, newly minted teens who were crazy enough to put their faces in the way of much larger fists. I convinced myself that given our ages we needed to arm ourselves as insurance. The Lord knows that my actual arm was not good for very much.

Chiddy looked like he was on a white sandy beach somewhere while our cohort grew ravenous. A lot of words were said until he snapped out of his mental vacation and scanned the frothing horde.

"I have learned that there are many ways to mess with a kid, and I am proud that we are all gathered here to handle this like men. I am proud. Now let's go get those weapons and meet back here for the show," Chiddy boomed. With that, our recruits scrambled fervently in all directions.

I wanted to argue. I could draw up a list of reasons as to why this new wrinkle was a bad idea, but what we had already achieved felt special.

I didn't want to fetch weapons, so I left the others and set off for the hobby shop. I walked past the girls' dormitory with its high walls and hidden secrets. They had a beautiful courtyard out front that would have never lasted on our side of campus. I strode past the medical center, where I often pretended to be sick since the nurses could give out meals outside of cafeteria hours. I cut through the laundry field, where wires upon wires of clotheslines rose from the ground, harboring all of our identical clothing. There was a long stretch of concrete at the end of the field where you could hand wash your clothes. I had done a lot of work for The Herd there. I almost tripped over a large green bucket that lay cracked in the grass. Someone had written "Uche's bucket" in black marker. I had been missing that bucket for months. I ended up at the hobby shop. The school paid kids who made desks and chairs. We broke the ones in our classrooms at an alarmingly fast rate.

I wrestled about whether to preach diplomacy as I returned to the soccer field. We could talk to The Herd. We could bluff them. We could fight them. The kids who respected me might come to think of me as a coward if I misspoke. The movies don't end in handshakes.

To give us credit, we often flirted with trouble. We snuck out of our cramped rooms after the 9:45 p.m. curfew to play cards in empty classrooms. One of us took charge of a hot iron and melted sugar smuggled from the cafeteria onto uncooked instant noodles. We broke away from the early morning jogging groups and played table tennis with broken roll-on deodorant balls in dorm hallways. We took to pranking Sarjo, the disciplinarian, at every possible turn. Sarjo was a former sergeant in the Nigerian military. He was tall and portly, but you needed a head start if you were to outrun him because he was quicker than advertised. Somehow it made perfect sense to us that a few eighteen-year-olds scared us way more than a cinderblock of a man who had been trained to kill people.

"Do you think one of these rods could crack someone's head open?" my friend Bravo pondered. Hair remover had been rubbed into his scalp in his sleep, and The Herd patted his bald head with Vaseline for weeks.

"I hope so," Little D chuckled. He was infamous for yanking shirts off of clotheslines. He ripped the name tag from the inner sleeves and wore each shirt until they got too dirty. The Herd had beaten the kleptomania out of him.

"Are you ready?" Chiddy asked, swinging an iron gently by its chord.

"No," I thought. "Yes!" I said.

"Good. Then we are off!" he cackled. The ugly crier usurped my leadership.

The gang poured off the field and cut past the chapel where we should have learned to turn the other cheek. We might have been daydreaming or gazing at girls in their Sunday dresses. I strained to stay at the front of a pack that was more interested in living out the Old Testament: an eye for an eye.

The Herd stood in a huddle by the bleachers of the outdoor basketball court. We expected, through a tip from Bravo, to find them there. He heard that they were to meet that evening to collect something from under the bleachers. At a guess, they were examining and dividing their stash. Chiddy pulled us to a halt by the sideline. I stood beside Chiddy on the edge of life as we knew it. He marinated in the moment.

All I really wanted was to fit into this community, to have boarding school be a home away from home. My father had clapped me on the back at the airport before I left for the first time and promised that I was leaving a boy to become a man. I moaned at the cliché of the moment. Once we leaked onto the court, we would become homeless men. The turbulence would never end.

The Herd saw us. Dapo, Ayo, Tobe, Obi, John, Shola, and Ben glared at us. Once we spread onto the court, everyone would inherit my predicament. They would look over their shoulders until their neck muscles wept. There would be no reprieve for the turbulence.

Chiddy put his wobbly arm up to signal that we were about to charge. I put a hand on his chest and pushed him back gently. I stared at Little D incredulously as I broke rank.

"Wait here," I ordered. The steel in my voice was irresistible. I cut the distance to The Herd in half. I cut the distance in half again and again and again. Dapo never broke eye contact. I remembered his fist.

"Enough is enough," I said. Other words spilled out of my mouth too, but I struggled to hear them over my beating heart. Various levels of surprise were painted on the faces of the seven members of The Herd. Standing against the backdrop of my vengeful, diminutive comrades, I waited for a response. My chin lifted, finding its proper nook in the air. My chin was reminded in the next instant that getting punched hurts. I heard a chorus of thuds and rattles that confused me since I had already hit the ground. Then came the pounding of what could only be an ensemble of kamikaze feet. I caught a glimpse of Chiddy hurtling clumsily my way. His hands were empty.

I tried. We made like musketeers.

February 3, 2013

5

Black Thunder

WE HAD ALL been strangers just a minute ago, but stepping into the arena melded us into a band of brothers. The beer on hand in clear plastic cups was a coconspirator in turning all of us nine-to-five pencil pushers into a drunken cult. Sandra stopped coming to the fights a long time ago. She felt queasy in the midst of a crowd that wanted blood as if we were transported to a Coliseum awaiting its gladiators. We all screamed in sync for Hank the Cutter.

I had always wanted to be a boxer, making my mother's face scrunch up at the thought of it, as if she had eaten a basket of lemons. Luckily for her, I was relegated to the sidelines because I just couldn't take a punch. This fact held true even as I lifted weights and funneled steaks. I watched a man get hit so hard that he traveled back to middle school. Another guy lost two teeth down his throat, coughed up blood and enamel, and laughed, "Good thing I have dental insurance!" All around me, men took punches that would have killed mere mortals. I wondered how they had the chins and the stomachs for it. Maybe they were all just crazy. Whatever it was, like being tall, I couldn't will the necessary traits into being. Instead, I was the guy whose mouse lay in the trash from being clicked into oblivion in pursuit of tickets to Shango's return fight. Now I yelled alongside a bunch of men whose mothers were probably just as happy that they stood by water coolers and not in squared circles.

My best friend, Stan, gambled on every fight. He watched from home, insisting that it was foolish to fly to Las Vegas when the best view came via high definition. I pictured him biting his nails and writhing on the couch as each round unfolded. He put money on every fight scheduled that night, watching clips of upstarts on YouTube to decide whom to place his faith in. Trainers and promoters scrambled to get their favored fighters on the undercard in order to get a slice of the money and recognition that a world heavyweight fight promised. One stellar performance could propel a man from working two jobs to pay for training to a level that meant that no one he knew would have to work again. A lot of handshakes were made in dark corners. The oddsmakers, the overlords, traipsed up and down the aisles, wearing consternation atop their suits.

Many reporters, often dressed more shabbily, wore similar expressions on their faces. They kept their money in their pockets but staked their professional reputations on analyzing the fights. Most proclaimed that Shango, the former world heavyweight champion of the world, was bound to lose because of his ring rust. "No tune-up fight? No chance," they declared. Almost all of the reporters were in the kind of shape that suggested they had never struck a punching bag in their lives. I had been different to my former brethren in that regard. I had become a freelance writer, but I was a full-time fan. Some of the reporters broke into wide grins of their own as fandom bounced out of their eyes. They all had their smartphones out to react to every fight on Twitter, the blogosphere, and on their websites in real time.

Only one of the three undercard bouts gave us the knockout we craved. As the last of the anonymous fighters made his way to the back, we fidgeted in our seats because we knew the main event was upon us. Even the ring girls, who knew where every camera was and when to smile into each of them, held their breath and stared up the entranceway.

Jay-Z's "The Ruler's Back" broke in the arena, but we ambushed the rapper's words with boos. As united as we had been in cheering for Hank, we might as well have become Voltron in the way we hurled our disdain for Shango. I had thought that such impassioned responses were extinct. Outside of this cauldron, most people stared blankly at me when I rambled on about shocking knockouts and controversial split decisions. I didn't think we would have the vitriol to do anything but take in Shango, the former poster boy of boxing, like a breath of fresh air. He had taken three years off to chase his dream of becoming an actor, but his detour had turned his supporters into jilted ex-lovers. The commissioner, Jamie Keane, demanded to know, six months into the hiatus, when his heavyweight champion of the world would agree to fight the number-one contender. Shango hemmed and hawed before forfeiting the title. That he draped the belt over Keane's shoulder stung more than my wife, Sandra, giving back my wedding ring ever could. I slept on Stan's couch for a week before I was forgiven for suggesting as much.

We all claimed to have boycotted the movies he appeared in, especially when he didn't even act in adrenaline-pumping action flicks. Shango pointed at his supermodel girlfriend, Maria, before putting a salami-sized finger to his lips, but his smile was painted on. His entourage charged ahead of him, hoisting banners with all of the brands that sponsored him. A man next to me spat, "No heart in that one. He is just in it for the money!" I had devoured all of his interviews, and all of his answers swirled in my head. He talked about gardening, winning a Tony, and watching shows on Netflix with his girlfriend. I wondered whether a ventriloquist was responsible for such responses. I couldn't put such talk next to quotes like "I want to put these cats in coffins," "I am everybody's worst nightmare," and "I like to head out to the ring first because I want my opponents to step out from the curtain and see what a god in his realm looks like." I remembered the menacing glares and snarls.

No one remembered how much time he'd spent recounting how dedicated he was to being the best boxer, too. He'd had the toughest training regimen and the strictest diet, even though he had always been the kind of specimen to whom a pair of gloves or a pigskin seemed ordained. His father was his first coach. "I have a bad wheel, son," he'd huffed, "but you have all the tools." His father grew up in Nigeria, but you couldn't make much money boxing there even if you mastered your craft. Scouts rarely came, and they certainly lacked the patience for a prospect with a knee damaged by a rash soccer tackle. To be both George Clooney and George Foreman, to live out both his and his father's dreams, was a step too far for us. We had no choice but to get in bed with another man.

That man was Hank the Cutter, our champion of convenience. He had a ginger beard that hid his Adam's apple and could have served as a great spot for a bird's nest. His face was pale and pockmarked, and his body, while sturdy, was not what one would call muscular. He looked like someone you could fire up the grill and drink beers with. While Shango was the template for how you wished you could box, Hank stood for how you would probably box if given the chance in reality. Given that, it was easy to dust him off and refashion him as our man. His kamikaze style of fighting turned from amateurish to endearing. The analysts stopped talking about how he never defended properly and hailed his intangibles. "Hank the Cutter has the heart of a champion! Hank has that 'never say die' attitude." His winning the heavyweight championship went from being lucky to being gritty.

There were whispers that his team crammed as many fights into his schedule as possible out of fear that idle time would tempt him into drinking whiskey and smoking cigars, among other things. Besides putting him out of fighting shape, they remembered both the assault charge he overcame and the drug ban he received as a result of his recreational habits early in his career. He still boasted about rolling the best joints for his friends. Because he was so open about such things, a microphone often turned into a powder keg. His heart raced whenever he got the chance to treat audiences to his unique blend of curse-laden sentences. He was in the business of knocking people out and didn't get caught up in being civil. This explained why he walked down to the ring with few sponsors to champion. Hank often heard that he was in a position to be a role model, which induced belly-aching laughter from him and his crew. He only began to consider his stature when the unfamiliar sounds of adoration began pouring in. The arena shook as he bounced down the entranceway with his team and drunken friends. His younger brother Ed led the procession, holding the heavyweight championship belt aloft in both hands.

Shango stood stoically in the ring, but we wanted him to give us energy to feed off of. He wore a pair of gloves that had famously popped up on Maria's Instagram, lying on the passenger seat of a Mercedes SLS. He slapped the gloves together twice before the two men came nose to nose in the center of the ring. One man was at ease and clean-shaven, while the other was manic and grizzly, bopping on his toes. One man had been on a red carpet a month ago, while the other had been living like Bear Grylls in the wilderness. He looked like a kid who had been dragged to visit an aunt on a Saturday afternoon. The ring girls, referee, and announcer often added to the aura of fights. On that night though, the girls prancing and parading around the ring, the referee gesticulating, and the announcer reverberating were excruciating buffers to a fight we could wait no longer to see. My hope for most fights was that they emulate the cooking of a good steak. We all wanted a juicy encounter, so the bout couldn't end too early or drag on too long and risk being overcooked.

When the bell finally rang, the crescendo was like thunder. With the din ringing in his ears, Shango's fists responded eloquently. Hank the Cutter's face quickly reminded me of why I could never be a boxer. His lip busted open, his eyes clamped shut, his ears turned to mush, blood fell down his face like an avalanche, and his cheek started to look like it was stowing away a jawbreaker. He fell to the canvas, writhed, and returned to his twitchy knees. Hank the Cutter threw punches gratuitously, but they seemed to only ricochet like bullets off of Superman Shango's chest. He then abandoned the idea of striking Shango and hoped only to survive, holding onto the monolith every chance he could. He slouched on the stool in his corner of the ring and dreamed of being in a La-Z-Boy chair. All the while, he spat pools of blood between his legs, protesting rising to the bell. The persistent cheers coaxed him out the corner.

The final decision was a mere formality. After bouts, most boxers acted as if the result had gone their way, raising their weary arm in the air like any credible victor would. Hank did not entertain this delusion as he sat on a stool beside Shango, the referee, and the announcer. His brother Ed placed a hand on his back while a ringside physician peered into each glassy eye with a flashlight. The scorecards read 120–106, 120–106, 120–104, and we booed when they were read. One of my new friends shrieked, "What a robbery!" Stan would be moping on his couch because he had put his money on Hank winning by way of knockout. The reporters jotted furiously, drafting ways to eat crow gracefully or constructing defenses of their critiques. The oddsmakers found themselves on the wrong side of the betting line. I was upset too because the fight sucked since only one guy had shown up.

There was to be no truce between that guy and the crowd. Shango ensnared the heavyweight championship in one hand and looked at us with a pained expression. There were cracks in the wall that he had put up. Maria stepped into the ring, and the two of them embraced. Almost all of her, from her curly black hair to her ample bottom, was enveloped in his arms. He shook his head afterward, touched her stomach for a couple of seconds, and stepped out of the ring without giving a speech. His trainer breathed, "We just want to thank God for believing in us when no one else did. This is not just a pay check for us. We love the sport of boxing, and it feels good to be the best in the world."

We didn't see or hear from Shango or his camp for days. The disappearing act of such a colossus was a trade secret that only the likes of Big Foot were privy to. In his absence, the pundits and talking heads erected a tombstone and shoveled dirt on the grave of his boxing career. They hissed about how he could have been the greatest boxer of all time if he had only applied himself better. They delved into the annals of history, evoked the names of legends, and spoke at length about how the best boxers clearly had different DNA than Shango. Shango himself was not around to defend himself or absorb the body blows as he did in the ring. I was relieved that I was no longer paid to give my opinion because I would have been forced to swim against a current that cried that a man of Shango's talents was obliged to maximize. The fans, even in the midst of booing, paid his mortgage and deserved better. That was how the story went. Everyone was myopic to the fact that Shango's boxing career was a product of buckets of sweat, that the fight could have and should have been stopped was a mere distraction.

Before long, Commissioner Keane was again waddling before a podium with the world heavyweight championship perched on his shoulder. I remembered Shango's finger to his lips and wondered whether we should have just enjoyed a master at work. I'd been in a turbulent on-again-off-again relationship in college and recognized the schizophrenic feelings of love, hate, regret, and rage. We said good riddance but refreshed the ESPN homepage in hope of news about his impending return.

The empty seats returned, and I started asking Sandra if she wanted to do other things on the weekend. I have to confess that it was good for the two of us. I learned things about her that I had never known or long since forgotten. Half a decade on from Shango's disappearance, she excitedly passed on a magazine article about hot new shows on Broadway. There was a picture of a burly man with a four-year-old girl in his arms. The caption read: "Reva Williams on fatherhood and finally achieving his wildest dreams!" He cracked a broad, toothy smile in the photo, and I realized that I had never seen Shango so elated before. Things were going according to plan—his, not ours.

Summer 2013

6

Poison Pill

IN THE AFTERMATH of another whirlwind press conference, Bill Barns sat slumped with his impotent, crumpled notes twisting in between his pair of Italian leather shoes. Sips of water did not arrest the bitter taste of agony squatting in his mouth. He had been wrong to continuously expose both himself and the pill to the battery of questions. Each dissent, lobbed his way like a grenade, had become more venomous. His ability to brush the doubts aside had deserted him under pressure. Cameras and tongues flickered at increasingly faster rates, fuelling a cacophony of snickering lights and run-on sentences. Microphones and tape recorders stretched toward him like slowed-down versions of boxer's jabs. The press conference was held in a small newsroom that could have felt cozy if the topic had been different. Bill, before a sea of seats and faceless suits, was engulfed in claustrophobia.

The euphoria had once been palpable over the small pink pill that allegedly measured true love. Those days had evaporated, leaving Bill to contend with a jilted and swelling mass who felt cheated and wanted blood. They challenged the science behind the pill, called the product a scam, chased potential customers away, and demanded a litany of answers and legal reprieves. That Bill Barns was still standing was a testament to the enduring, insatiable curiosity of so many. Fear and confidence snared couples, who worried about broken homes and marriages; who believed in fairy tales and romantic movies and seemed immune to bad publicity - putting the pill in the same rarified air as packs of cigarettes.

Bill's Rolex watch, tailored suits, and immaculately slick hair all reeked of a man enjoying success. Sitting hunched, drenched in silence, Bill craved a cigarette for the first time in over twenty years. He wouldn't cave, just as he wouldn't cave when it came to keeping the pill they called Lovanol alive. He needed to invent a new, compelling argument to stem the tides of discontent.

"Mr. Barns? You are running late for your next scheduled appointment," a voice called out. Bill looked up and saw that a blond head had crept its way back into the room. The head belonged to his secretary, Sarah Miller. His face flooded with relief. He was rescued from his thoughts. Together they made their way out of the cauldron. Bill stared expectantly at Sarah, waiting for her to say, "I told you so," for deciding to host a press conference, to put himself at the mercy of a gaggle of ravenous reporters. Sarah said very little to Bill, as she batted away stray reporters along their march toward his driver and black Mercedes.

Bill wanted to loosen his tie to make more room for gulping Scotch. The coming appointment could not compete with the idea of diving under his duvet and the sheets of an innumerable threat count below. He thought about intimating to Sarah that he wanted to abscond, but he knew she would scold and stare holes through him with her saucerlike blue eyes. She read his mood anyway.

"Buck up. The meeting with Mr. Eze could be a turning point," she offered.

The name ignited a spark of optimism. While many wanted Barns to disappear forever, fans existed who lauded him and brought success stories to his attention. A man called Emeka Eze had written him a letter dripping with the kind of romanticism that could instantly inspire someone to hoist a blaring boom box outside of his lover's window. Sarah watched as his radiant grin, absent as of late, surfaced upon the recollection of Emeka Eze and his scrawled words. She was glad because Bill's veneer of youth had begun to fade until then.

Sarah marveled at her boss's enduring belief in the concept of love. Her boss was a fifty-two-year-old survivor of three divorces. He thought he had been in love with all three of his wives but swore in hindsight that he had been wrong each time. "I was seduced by the idea of love and clutched at mirages," he huffed in private and boomed in promotional speeches. "I needed protection from my naiveté," he continued in his reflection on how a pill like Lovanol could have saved him from himself. Bill challenged all listeners to be responsible. "Make sure you are not in a relationship under false pretenses. Make sure you are in the relationship you deserve." For a time he had the masses nodding with him as if marionettes controlled their heads. Few could argue that something needed to be done about the rising divorce rate. Bill Barns was hailed as the crusader out to save the purity of marriage.

They pulled up to a four-story office complex. Bill Barns was the CEO of Modern Pharmaceuticals, whose only product was Lovanol. Modern Pharmaceuticals' office was a hybrid creature that ran in part like a clinic. People had the option of taking the pill at home, but many chose to visit the office, to have their results reviewed by professionals. They were driven to the office by the doubt or confidence that drove most people to Lovanol.

Bill grimaced again as the car came to a stop in the parking lot. A smattering of picketers huddled around the entrance, harassing staff and customers alike with their signs and petitions. Bill prevented security from ever chasing them away.

"We are not scared of their voices," he argued. He knew to put his blinders on so as not to have his day ruined, but one placard marched into his line of sight. A tall, elderly man hoisted a sign high above his head that read, "Lovanol killed my forty years of marriage!" in deep red marker. Bill recognized the man. His name was Earl. He had a short, graying Afro and an ever-growing beard that he sarcastically called his "protest beard." Earl was known to carry a stack of business cards for the Pill Support Group. Given how often he came to protest, Bill wondered if he was homeless, but Earl came dressed in vibrant polo shirts, khaki trousers, and an array of nice-looking loafers. Sarah pulled at Bill's arm and once again ploughed through the group of dissenters.

They plunged into the office, which was not an overwhelmingly large building. The company was five years old and of little significance until the emergence of Lovanol just over a year ago. Customers who came in were tested on the first floor. The other floors, from the second to the fourth floor, were where business and research took place. Bill's office was on the uppermost floor adjacent to that of the CTO, Aditya Patel. Aditya dedicated himself to R & D projects that never came to fruition. Bill left Aditya to his own devices though, because protecting Lovanol had become his all-encompassing priority.

Emeka Eze sat in the conference room, wolfing air in a fight to catch his breath. He had gotten caught up in preparing his anniversary gift for Roselyn and found himself atop his bicycle, spinning his legs like an out-of-control Ferris wheel in order to get to the appointment on time. He'd awkwardly cradled the gift in his left arm while groping the right handlebar. Emeka had had no time to change, wearing his gray college sweatshirt, faded yellow T-shirt, and cut-up jeans. His shoes were scuffed, and his helmet left his small Afro contorted. After pulling up to the office, he'd jogged toward the building. A picketer had intercepted him at the entrance and jammed a business card into his hand. The card was white with a black broken heart on one side. The other side read "Pill Support Group" with the e-mail address "psg@gmail.com" underneath.

"Contact us when they break your heart too," the elderly picketer, wearing a green Lacoste polo, had croaked.

Emeka tapped the business card against the conference table. He had written Bill Barns to both thank him and share how he was going to pay tribute to his girlfriend with Lovanol. He had not expected a reply, but a cursive hand-written letter had come in the mail from a Sarah Miller on behalf of Bill Barns. He'd been asked to come to the Modern Pharmaceuticals office at his earliest convenience. Bill sat at his desk, reading Emeka's letter over and over again. His phone danced off the hook incessantly, cutting every thought off from blossoming. Shareholders wanted to discuss the failed press conference.

"The phone calls can wait," he snapped.

"OK. Then, Mr. Eze is waiting for you in the conference room," Sarah replied.

He gave her a nod and made his way to meet the young romantic.

Emeka's hand disappeared in Bill's grasp, but the handshake was surprisingly gentle. Bill flashed a smile that made him feel like he had just put on a fur coat in the winter. Bill was portly, in a hearty way, and his eyes lit up like the lights in Las Vegas. Television did not do the towering six-feet-five man justice.

"I read your letter many times. Your Roselyn sounds like a great lady, so I am happy for you, Mr. Eze. I am in this business because of people like you. I get a kick out of couples basking in the knowledge of finding true love. All I offer is knowledge," Bill said. Emeka nodded fervently. He was about half as old as Bill and younger than all but one of Bill's four children. Emeka looked like an undergraduate to Bill, and he thought for a second that the man before him might not be mature enough for his freshly formed proposal. At Emeka's age, Bill toted a briefcase and wore a suit every day like the quintessential businessman that he had hoped to become. Emeka was clearly a very different person, but what was important was that he exuded the confidence of someone who had been let in on the big secret. There was only assuredness when he spoke about Roselyn Yu.

"I asked you here, Mr. Eze, because I think we can help each other out. I see us forming a partnership of sorts, and I hope you will find my proposal agreeable. I believe in the love that you and Roselyn share, and I want to showcase it. I have come to understand your anniversary plans, and I want to document the whole thing. You are in a position to be an inspiration to lovers around the world. You can motivate lovers who want to find what you have found with Miss Yu. You can show them what it feels like when two people learn they are meant to be together forever."

Written testimonies, paid actors, and his speaking on behalf of the product all helped, but nothing compared to exposing the public to a genuine experience. Bill Barns explained that he wanted to make a television special out of Emeka and Roselyn's Lovanol experience. They would film the days before their fifth anniversary. They would capture them at the office, taking the pill under professional supervision. They would record the two of them exchanging gifts in honor of their five years together. They would shoot them opening the envelopes containing the results from taking the pill. Finally, they would immortalize the moment when Emeka got on one knee and proposed to Roselyn. Bill was prepared to let the young man think it over, but in a matter of moments, Emeka shot his hand out and it disappeared once again into Bill's obliging soft massive enclave of a palm. The handshake they shared was firmer than the first one, as if to say the deal was sealed.

Once outside, Emeka wanted to run to Roselyn to share everything with her. He knew she would be at Starbucks, surrounded by cappuccinos and textbooks. The pill intrigued her, and she saw no harm in taking it although she was not an ardent believer in the product herself. If he burst into Starbucks, blabbering about his meeting with Bill Barns, he could see her laughing gently at him over her volumes on the law. Emeka did not trust himself to keep his cool. He would also have to answer questions about the rectangular object draped in a purple, silk cloth, her secret gift.

"What have you got there?" Emeka's roommate Tobe yelled from the kitchen as Emeka swung the apartment door open and strode into his room. Tobe looked away from the plantains he was frying and waited impatiently for a response from his animated friend.

"I met Bill Barns. Roselyn and I are going to take the pill, and they are going to record us," Emeka boomed from the bedroom.

Tobe pulled the frying pan off the burner and entered the room to raise his concerns. Emeka's lair was littered, to say the least. In particular, comic books, both pristine and weathered and of all genres, formed multiple stacks in the room. Panels from certain issues had been torn out and plastered on the walls. Emeka was twenty-six years old, but he got a pass in Tobe's mind because he was a comic-book artist for African Creative Comics. His bedroom doubled as his place of work. Emeka would often chuckle, saying, "My mess brings me my mojo."

"That sounds romantic," Tobe deadpanned. He had followed the plan from its infancy when it seemed like a carelessly tossed out idea until now, and it had never struck him as a sensible thing to do. His friend had always listened to his heart before anything else. Emeka was a chemical-engineering major who had bucked reason to start an independent comic-book outfit. Tobe had admired that. This was different.

"You should call your pops and ask him what he thinks about this," Tobe suggested.

"I am going to propose to her."

"Then you should really call your father."

Emeka smiled back. He wore a similar expression every time they talked about his fascination with the pill. Emeka had drawn up the perfect way to get engaged. Debates were unnecessary.

"I will announce the good news when we are engaged in a week," Emeka chuckled. Tobe left in resignation, and Emeka began barreling around the room, collecting every item that evoked memories of his relationship with Roselyn. "The camera crew is coming later today!" he yelled.

⸺⸺⸺

A week later, Roselyn and Emeka were sitting with Bill Barns, Aditya Patel, and Sarah Miller in what resembled a private hospital room. Roselyn marveled at how they had achieved such a sense of sterility. Aditya and Bill wore white research coats. Roselyn and Emeka had each brought a box full of tokens from their relationship.

"Miss Yu, please follow me to the room next door," Aditya announced. A cameraman trailed behind. Roselyn stuck her tongue out and cocked her eyebrows in Emeka's direction before blowing him a kiss. He watched her leave in her red-and-orange sundress. "Dress for success," she had giggled with a twirl after coming to his apartment to pick him up in her car.

"I am sure you know the drill," said Bill. "We will place sensors against your head and heart and then ask that you take this Lovanol pill. One by one, I will pull articles out of the box that you brought and request that you talk about them. You will need to think completely about the memories and stories you tell me and about the significant other behind them. You should soon feel the combined sensation of butterflies in your stomach, an accelerated heartbeat, and a slight whizzing in your head. All of these feelings are safe. In fact, they are ideal because they represent a positive result. In simple terms, the pill will accentuate the testosterone, estrogen, dopamine, norepinephrine, serotonin, oxytocin, and vasopressin in your body if your significant other triggers the release of these chemicals. Sometimes, individuals won't experience these phenomena or will falsely convince themselves that they did experience them. The sensors will reliably confirm or deny the actual result. As a result, coming to us to take the pill is a smart but by no means mandatory decision." Stress lines creased Bill's face after he spoke. Emeka had to concentrate so as not to glance at the camera.

Bill pulled out two ticket stubs to a 50 Cent show, and the sensations washed over Emeka immediately. Emeka clutched at his stomach and twitched sporadically for an instant. Bill recognized the telltale signs, and the two men cracked smiles. He looked to Sarah, who shrugged back at him with her arms folded. The reaction seemed to come too quickly in her mind. She wondered whether viewers would say it was staged. They would have to wait for the data from the sensors to be processed. Bill pulled out a couple more items from the box in the name of due diligence. Time had stood still ever since the meeting with Emeka.

Emeka, Bill, and Sarah waited outside of the room next door. Bill was staring at his watch when Roselyn emerged with a warm smile draped across her face. She pulled away a hair tie to release her shiny black hair.

"That was fun for something that does not matter," she quipped.

"Did you say that in there?" Bill asked.

"No, not all," she clucked.

"Good. We will send the official results in a couple of hours to each of your addresses," Aditya chimed in. Bill peeled off the research jacket and handed it to a passing employee. He clapped Emeka on the shoulder and left with Sarah, roaring over his shoulder, "If everyone is feeling good about things, I think we will air the anniversary dinner live."

Emeka blabbered in the car.

Summer 2013

7

Garage-Band Blues

Rod, scraggily bearded with eyes sunken from writing songs all night, strummed the guitar feverishly, yanking at the strings to realize his hopes for them. The amp underneath his foot screeched at its abuse, as the roar of electric guitar trampled eardrums. Scott and Rachel were his only audience, holding hands, heads lowered, but Rod played with a verve that was suited for stadia. Then, abruptly, the music stopped, and he shoved an arm deep into his book bag and retrieved a packet of cigarettes and a Zippo lighter.

They all stood in silence for a moment, as Rod scrutinized them in between puffs. The jet-black had been washed out of Rachel's hair, revealing an all-American blonde whom he had never known existed. Scott had cut his shoulder-length ratty hair down to an immaculately lined Caesar; they were both wearing suits, with briefcases resting against their ankles.

Rod had heard they were leaving the band, walking away from him and Toto, a chubby, lazy stoner who doubled as the best drummer Rod had ever heard. Rod had stayed up all night to perfect the chords he had just played, to prove that their potential as a group was too great to abandon, but it was immediately clear he had failed.

After ten years of clawing to make it as a successful act, Scott and Rachel had decided to retreat into the boredom of normal life. They repeatedly pleaded that they had a daughter to think about, as if all of the musical greats before them had been impotent or negligent parents. Cramming into Toto's hot-boxed minivan with their equipment to drive from gig to gig was being replaced by staring at a computer screen, monotonously tapping keys to perform insignificant tasks. Rod promised that once their daughter could comprehend him, he would look her in the eye and tell her that her father was once great but had forever lost the spine to chase his dreams. Scott would probably be seated in a modest living room, drinking beer and watching Monday Night Football. There was nothing wrong with that, but there was nothing amazing either.

Then Toto burst in, panting violently, with a box of pizza and what looked to be a bag of mushrooms resting on it. "For old times' sake!" he roared.

Rod screamed, "Fuck that!" and stormed out with an expertly rolled blunt dangling between his fingers. He would get high by himself. He would do everything by himself.

November 16, 2011

8

A Minivan for One

ROD GAVE THE garage a final look over, turned the lights off, and forced the rusted front door shut. The loud rattle of metal signaled that there would be no going back—the decision to leave was now final. Head down, he trudged toward a dull gray minivan parked on the sidewalk, in which he had placed nothing but his trusted electric guitar.

He had owned the instrument for close to fifteen years, from when he was a pimply-faced, shy teenager who only dared to play as far removed from earshot as possible. Then, as always, a girl had changed everything. She'd invaded the garage when his soul was exposed, strumming the chords to a hopelessly awful song he had written. He had forgotten that he had invited her to come and work on homework questions to which he knew the answers, and he stopped and gawked at her, feeling naked. He'd thought she would laugh and scurry away to embarrass him, but she'd egged him on, filling his head with the idea that he was good and that the world needed to hear him play.

"You are the best ever," she'd gushed, and driven by her hyperbole, Rod had formed a band with her and his best friends, Toto and Scott. He had clung onto Rachel's notion that he, and by extension the band, had something to offer the masses. But, no tangible success had materialized, and the group had fractured under the weight of unfulfilled dreams.

"Wait!" a voice bellowed, as a heavyset man with an uncombed, splaying Afro lumbered up the street. He stopped, panting heavily, wolfing in air and clawing sweat off of his forehead while resting the other hand against his knee. Rod stared at his best friend Toto and smiled meekly. He was happy that perhaps someone had come to talk him out of leaving, as he had feared that no one would care enough to do so. Maybe that was why he had taken so long to comb over the house and garage when he knew beforehand that all he was going to take with him was the electric guitar, his songbook, and his mother's Polaroid camera. This last was surprisingly still a coveted possession, as Rod always declared that he had to document their legacy, their ride to the top, as much and as often as possible. Oftentimes, the photos filled in the blanks of the booze-filled nights, joyriding across the city in their minivan. Now he would have to do it all without them because Toto, Rachel, and Scott had given up. They called it "growing up".

Even after his most obnoxious moments (like when whiskey drunk he had puked on spectators during a show or launched himself into crowds to fight hecklers), his close friends supported him. They turned him onto his side when he passed out, they helped him write curse-filled odes to girls who rejected him, and when his mother fell ill, they held his hand and turned away to let him sneak out the tears. Each of them had propped him up, but when you punch out one of your best friends and declare you are going to become a star—come hell or high water—you either have to apologize or back up your words. Rod had never learned to do the former; his friends had always done it for him.

With over thirty years to collect wisdom, Rod knew that much of the rift was petty and immature, but it was not hard for him to convince himself that Scott—the charming, square-jawed heartthrob—had deserved being struck. He played the bass guitar, strumming the chords that Rod fed him, singing the vocals that Rod penned too; but worse than the coasting was the fact that he had stolen both Rachel's heart and her desire to perform with him, Rod. Scott ticked all the boxes that make for a good, wholesome man; he could afford to step away and get by as an average Joe. Without music though, Rod was just a gangly, thorny shell of a character—one who drank too much, indulged in too many drugs, and showed too much neglect for hygiene. His persona was very much incongruent with the rules, so entertaining them was not an option. If it came down to it, he would play bingo halls, bar mitzvahs, and street corners. He would crash karaoke competitions, too, if he had to, but, as was tattooed on his stomach, he would "Never Conform."

Maybe if he had not thought to squeeze beside Rachel on the school bus and lie that he was terrible at trigonometry, he would have graduated from a fancy place like Harvard, the way his mother said he would. Maybe.

As fate would have it, Toto, the garage, and everything he knew were left in the minivan's rearview, abandoned as they had abandoned him, and he was going to get high, get cozy in a strip club, and scribble the lyrics that would change his life. Or at a minimum, he would give his future some actual thought in the state of mind in which he worked best.

November 20, 2011

9

Don't Forget the Fireworks—First Person

I HAD SPENT my entire life hoping for a night like that, where a girl would look at my pimpled face and gangly frame and want its limbs to fold around her. A pulled muscle and an overflowing scrapbook of awkwardness later, though, what I felt was unbridled disappointment.

I should have been happy because being there, on her absurdly high-thread-count Egyptian-cotton sheets, was a dream I had replayed in my mind for eons. I read more *Playboy* than novels, prepping myself mentally for the day that I prayed would come. Nothing prepared me, though, for how Kristen stared apishly at me, opening her mouth in a small O shape to speak before restraining herself and sealing her lips again. I could see her grappling to put the narrative together, and then her eyes trembled as understanding flooded in. The bottle of sangria we had stolen from her parents' cabinet, my sweating to decipher the code that was her bra hook, the clashing of nobly knees, and the fumbling for hidden crevices: our pieces just did not fit, like playing Tetris drunk, and my mind worked feverishly to figure out how I could excuse myself.

"You should use the window," she muttered, unable to hold my gaze while she synced to my present thoughts in a way that had been painfully absent the night before.

I bobbled my head in agreement and picked up my clothes, as well as any vestiges of decency I could find on the ground. My jacket had gone missing though, so the cold snickered at me as I trudged all the way home in my tank top.

I had always thought that there would be fireworks, that I would hear my soul cry tears of joy, and that together we would create love. Instead, I would have to settle for chest bumps from friends, girls whispering incessantly when I walked by, and the torn, sticky packet sliding in my pocket as a memento. I did have a box of fireworks at home though, but gone were the days when I could call my buddy Tim and salvage the day by setting them off.

November 6, 2011

10

Don't Forget the Fireworks—Third Person

CHUCK WOKE UP to find himself in the fetal position that had been forced upon him, as Kristen lay splayed in all directions, snoring loudly and gobbling up all the space on the bed. He stared at her svelte, bare frame and wondered how a night filled with so much promise had gone awry.

Her makeup was smeared against the pillow, and parts of an eyelash dangled precariously. She then yawned, and her eyes fluttered open, rattled by the site of Chuck's pimply mug an inch away from hers. He was not the knight she had always envisioned carrying her over the threshold in burly arms, and the pounding in her head told her to blame the sangria.

Chuck was of no help, gawking like a lost puppy, but in his face she could see some of the innocence that had snuck up on her and drawn her to him. Innocence had been extinguished and replaced by adult affairs, and, having never let a boy see her in her unfiltered state, she knew he had to leave immediately. The window would have to do because she could not risk him walking by her parents.

Chuck, rendered dumb, slowly gathered his belongings, almost in a trance, before meekly shuttling out of the window in a beer-soaked tank top and jeans. The harsh wind outside would cut through his lanky frame and probably induce pneumonia, but as Kristen watched him descend out of sight, her thoughts were dominated by what her friends would say when they heard about the encounter. Moments later, her heart yelled in terror, as it dawned on her that the jacket he was unable to find could be anywhere in the house, anywhere her mother could stumble upon, and then all hell would break loose like adolescents with fireworks.

November 6, 2011

11

You Will, She Will

YES, I KNOW you are excited.

You have forgotten how to take breaths between sentences, and I can see your heart swelling. You want to run outside like a six-year-old and yell to the world that you have won, but if you do not sit still and listen to me, you will have your head in your hands wondering how everything crumbled so quickly. I cannot count the number of times I have worn your shoes; they must be so threadbare on you by now.

Here is the thing. Yes, she sounds amazing, but you have to wait before you pick up that phone and call her. How long? At least three days, and they will be three of the longest, hardest days of your life. Am I exaggerating? You wish. Everything you do and see will remind you of her. English will feel like gibberish because her voice, lounging in your head, will drown the world out. You will convince yourself that you have never heard anything so sweet before; you will find yourself strangling your phone in the hope that by some miracle it will ring and her voice will walk into your ear. She will not call you. You'll type useless, long-winded text messages that, to you, feel like sonnets, and your nerves will fall off a cliff as you grapple with whether to hit "Send." That text, revised more than your final term paper, will be passed from friend to friend for approval, and the powerful computer on your lap will groan at the middling task of cycling through her Facebook photos. You will dream about the day that you will see yourself in them, tagged, the two of you pulling cute faces with her hand braided in your sweaty palms. Oh, trust me! You have the sweatiest palms in this world. Worst of all, you will look in the mirror, and the hairstyle that you have adored your entire life will feel juvenile and inadequate. You will question how your breath smells and your shirt looks—every three seconds. In short, these three days will be torturous, magical, the worst, the best, but all in all well worth the wait. So do just that. Wait. You don't understand? OK, let's try again.

You like her, but it is never that simple because showing her that you like her kills it all. You are 150 pounds monsoon wet, your biggest talents are playing *Mario Kart* and spitting long distances, and the farthest you have ever traveled in this world is to my house. I love you, but there is no obvious reason for her to even like you. If you do not call her though, all of a sudden she is the maiden at the window waiting for her hero to come calling. For all she knows, you are off slaying dragons while we will, in fact, be sitting in our boxers and eating stale pizza that tastes like cardboard while playing FIFA. She will be hooked on you because you are not like all the other guys, lining up, like it's Walmart on Black Friday, to talk to her. Nuisances. She will lunge at her phone whenever she hears a buzz, but it will only be a fly whispering in her ear, mocking her that you are busy on some adventure. She will stare at the wardrobe that she spent a lifetime building and reject it all, marching off to find a newer, tighter dress. She will scratch her head until the nail polish starts to chip off, wondering why she ever dated the football players, starving artists, and general riffraff when a man like you existed. Then, when she has almost given up, you will finally call her, and every ring will swallow a bit more of your confidence. Have no fear though, because she will pick up after an appropriate delay and give you the answer she has rehearsed:

"Oh, hello, Rick. Oh, is it Nick? ………… OK, I guess I could go out to dinner on Friday night."

Inside, your heart will tear at the thought that she is not excited, that she is throwing you a bone because saying no would have been too awkward, but you don't realize she is actually doing cartwheels.

In a perfect world, she would run outside too, jump and click her heels like she did oh-so-many years ago, and thumb her nose at the girls who look in your direction. The pity is that she has to be a secret agent, a mystery until the time is right. We do not blurt out what we really think or how we really feel. Then the celebration begins. You will slap my hand, I will wipe the sweat off on your shirt, and the cycle will start over. You will not be allowed to talk to her until that Friday; but by then you will be a seasoned veteran at this, and the time will fly by.

Oh no! Who are you texting? Her? Are you out of your mind?

She texted you back? But that only took a minute. What did she say?

She wants to meet tonight? But it is *Call of Duty* night. She must be desperate. Something is wrong with her. Something is definitely wrong with her, so be careful and wipe that smile off your face. Yes, I am only a year older than you, but I peaked early—remember? Junior high was a rager.

October 30, 2011

12

Frenetic Muscat

A STARVING, WIMPY "wadi dog" burst through an open construction site, yelping feebly for attention, but the workers in blue overalls ignored it, absorbed in the task at hand.
A building lay naked, scaffolding exposed, as men shuttled
mounds of dirt and cement to and fro. Muscat was a city ex-
ploding into life, demanding to be recognized as a place where
things happened. The rate of growth was frenetic. The workers
crammed into tents when night fell, serenaded by the croaks of
their hungry guest.

Across the wadi, men adorned in white *dishdashas* sat outside together to eat shawarmas, smoke *shisha*, and watch international soccer games shown on large projectors. They enjoyed
the cool evening under the city's bright lights, as they exhaled
clouds that hung lazily over them until the drone of engines

rattled their ears. A parade of vehicles from places they could only now dream of sailed by, and young men thrust their heads out of windows and sunroofs, giving their best growls of opulent victory. The big question was always whether or not the peacock ritual would work. Would the girls gathered in vibrant national dress, who together looked like a moving rainbow, or even the girls from faraway lands, be impressed?

The elderly men drinking Arabic coffee in the café window shook their heads and remembered the days when young people fished with their fathers and sold their catch at the souk. They hissed at the onslaught to the senses and wandered down to the market, where the women in their head dresses, with arms covered in intricate henna, sold jewelry, frankincense, and decorative boxes to tourists and Omanis alike. The foreigners in particular stopped at every stall and stared wide-eyed at the wondrous items that they had not known existed before. Artful at bargaining, one of the women waved a curved ceremonial dagger, a *khanjar*, and a crowd of onlookers gravitated toward her.

When work was done and treasures had been accumulated, the boys took to open fields and kicked soccer balls together at "goalposts" outlined by carefully arranged shoes. Thank goodness that still happened.

The graying men went to bed early before the streets truly morphed into an eclectic ensemble of locals and foreigners, all looking to dance and drink. The caution shown during the day, where alcohol was carted in unmarked brown boxes that one could pack a life in, was keenly discarded. When the bass finally retreated, the night owls stumbled down placid streets at four in the morning, with no cars or people in sight. Orange-and-white taxis were the only ones standing, enjoying their most profitable hours. At the same time, the men in blue overalls rose to clothe the scaffolds so that Muscat could continue to grow at its frenetic pace.

October 23, 2011

13

Death and Laughter: The Best of Friends

THE LINE THAT had snaked around the block disintegrated, as people peeled off in varying directions. A crowd had been waiting anxiously for MC Death Machine's autograph signing, but that is not what we witnessed that evening.

With sunglasses cloaking his eyes, and a sweeping, black, studded trench coat, Death Machine had boisterously leaped out of a small, white van and basked in the roars and adulation that his appearance demanded. My fingernails had been chewed raw, and I juggled all the questions that I wanted to ask him, hoping he would remember me from his other shows, photo shoots, and signings. In a perfect world, I would be a member of the media crew, microphone and notepad in hand, to interview him on behalf of my magazine. I laughed to myself thinking about what my mother would say at the thought of me skipping my actual job to wait for hours for Death Machine; I would have sunk any amount of time to see him.

Death Machine had revolutionized rap music, ushering in the new hybrid genre of metal rap. Sunken eyed and heavily tattooed, his work apprehended my heart and soul, capturing the harsh realities of the world in a way that was unparalleled. He transported me from the afternoons spent at the family record store, leaving me numb to my father's pleas to focus and cooperate, as I recycled his lyrics in my head. In short, Death Machine was everything to me, and as I looked at him, it almost appeared as if he had three eyes. He was that unreal.

With the crowd hollering as loudly as they were, I failed to hear the gunshot, but I saw his body jerk as if controlled by a drunken marionette. He crumpled to the floor, a death too quick for facial expressions. His music had stymied many people, and calls had been made to ban him in numerous states, but those details did not soften the shock of seeing that someone had shot him. Scrambling fanatics shoved me to and fro, and I listlessly obliged them, suddenly lost in memories of sitting on construction scaffolding with my ex-boyfriend Joey. I often rested a boom box on my lap while he bopped his head awkwardly, pretending to enjoy the blaring metal rap as he bossed steel beams and girders. With my toes dangling over the precarious edge of a budding skyscraper, I was made keenly

PAUL UCHE

aware of the fine lines between life and death. I would have plummeted to the pavement below if I hiccupped too heavily. At that, I laughed again, but this time it was hearty and out loud. I remembered how Death Machine had ultimately ended Joey and me and effectively supplanted Joey. From across the street, an elderly lady stared at me, wrought with confusion and terror at how I could find anything funny in the midst of the unraveling scene.

I remained rooted to the spot for an embarrassingly long time. Yellow caution tape sprang up and paramedics performed their formalities. My stomach soon protested over its neglect, so I finally extracted myself for the slow pilgrimage home. I was by no means excited, as all I had in my cubicle of an apartment was expired milk and leftover Chinese food. Solace would come from crawling into my hammock and listening to MC Death Machine; then it suddenly dawned on me why his death had not jarred my senses.

The man would live on. Immortalized in song, musicians never really die. We scrutinize, lean on, and ask more of them as each day passes until we ourselves wrinkle and keel over—or get shot. Excitement bubbled within me, and with no money for either the subway or a taxi, I sprinted all the way back, a gothic black blur running into the arms of her lover, idol, and best friend.

October 2, 2011

14

Being Is a Contact Sport

COLD BEADS OF sweat slowly trickled down the side of my head, tickling my cheeks before dripping carelessly onto the ground. My hands quivered violently as I inhaled air deeply, eyes scrunched shut in order to focus. The roars of an expectant, raucous crowd pelted my eardrums, and I slowly dared to lift my eyelids, taking in the most wondrous of sights. A swollen mass of people had come in droves to see me perform, and subsequently, feeling strong flickers of renewed confidence, I leaped off of the turnbuckle, challenging gravity to arrest my motion.

I expected to then hear cheers, but I was instead greeted with a harsh crescendo, as my beloved audience receded into the distance. All I could see were two pillars standing over me, as I lay sprawled out on the floor, a mess more hapless than discarded old toys. Looking up, I gaped in awe at the looming structures that quickly morphed into familiar faces. Heads shook, fingers wagged, and disappointment washed over all of our faces. One of the pillars smelled like sweat and grass and was clutching a glistening new trophy. The other's waft was an eclectic mix of musky cologne, brand new leather, and traces of coffee, wielding a briefcase that reeked of importance. Out of breath, I rambled to the giants, stumbling to explain the vision I had fashioned for myself.

I needed lipstick-red spandex pants, silver hoop-shaped earrings, and diamond-encrusted sunglasses. I was going to travel the world, grace magazine covers, and conduct interviews while clenching a remorseless steel chair that would warn all of my enemies. I was only a packed bag away from realizing this dream, but the pillars remained stern and unanimated, disinterested in my revelation. They did not grasp that I had been training feverishly and that by jumping off of sofas, I had morphed into Shawn Michaels, capable of hitting picture-perfect elbow drops. Then, on cue, blood began leaking out of the soon-to-be-famous elbow, and my budding excitement evaporated.

Gingerly, the well-dressed pillar scooped me up into its arms. "You are way too reckless," it proclaimed, while tampering with my limp, wounded elbow. Crimson streaks scurried in all directions.

"You are not Spiderman, you know. You can't act like a television character," the sweaty pillar chimed in, and my eyes popped open like saucepans, burning holes through each of them.

While they were able to pose as skyscrapers, I would not look out of place next to Frodo or Yoda. But, in my mind, I was king, and being king was a contact sport. I could not gallop down the flank of a soccer field, holding off defenders at will the way the sweaty pillar did; I did not know the answers to everything or complete successful business deals like the briefcase pillar did either; but I had a weapon unbeknownst to them. I owned an unparalleled imagination, and its cruel will was my command. Every fall that made me yelp, every bruise that made me wince, and every cut that made me cry proved that I was Bruce Willis's successor, gritty enough to stand back up and ask for more. I was Super Mario in pajamas, the little guy who could.

The sweaty pillar, my brother, pinned a hot towel against my gash, looking into my eyes with a concern that expected me to squirm and squeal. Instead I brushed off the pangs of pain and dismissed as child's play the ruby stains on the towel, the carpet, and my pajamas. I only felt the satisfaction of another challenge conquered, and the whites of my teeth refused to go away while they bandaged and warned me about my careless ways. Disinfectants, scissors, and gauze expertly darted in and out of sight; when the patch work was done, I sprang to my feet and dashed away, propelled by thoughts of who and what I could be next. Indiana Jones, Muhammed Ali, and Luke Skywalker tumbled through my mind, and my eyes grew manic at the possibilities. I would endeavor to wake up early the next day and spend it training to be anyone or anything I could conjure up.

"Go to sleep right now, you crazy person!" my father bellowed behind me, before breaking into a betraying, huge grin. I chuckled and stared back at my pillars, and for a brief moment, I considered that I could one day be like them, a pillar too. They in turn watched their daredevil charge and exchanged a glance that said it all.

I would be returning to their treatment table soon.

September 11, 2011

15

Bathrooms Are Black Holes

M Y MOTHER ALWAYS called at seven in the morning to ask how the day before had gone. Empty-nest syndrome had hit her hard, compounded by concern over a son that was a continent away. My body's protests at being woken early caused me to grumble nearly inaudible answers, reciting the things that she hoped to hear from time zones adrift. I painted tales of how I had gone to sleep early after doing all of my homework far ahead of time. A button-down shirt and trousers were finely ironed, starched, and laid out, and I made sure to eat fruit and take vitamins before leaving early for classes. I could almost hear her beaming on the other end of the phone, nodding in approval at how I appeared to conduct myself.

As the ritual recycled, I often felt the urge to deviate from it by fielding questions of my own, about my real life, but shedding those shackles made my teeth jangle. As far as my mother was concerned, I was a well-oiled machine, focused purely on collegiate success. Saying anything else would shatter her perfect picture, but I took the leap one day by failing to answer her inquiries properly. Matters wracked my mind, which forced me to release the biggest question of all.

"Why do girls go to the bathroom together?" I blurted.

My mother was seldom lost for words, but I had caught her off guard. Out of her element, she stuttered repeatedly, and awkward pauses lapped up time on the phone. In a bid to relieve her of her growing anxiety, I explained why the question was so pertinent to my life.

My hair had been a mess, my glasses were smudged, and the moustache I had fashioned was ripe for a stand-up comedian's jabs. My friend wore a poncho made out of a ratty, once white T-shirt and stumbled onto the dance floor in pink plastic sunglasses. We bumped into sweat-soaked patrons as thundering music abused our ability to think. Clumsily looking for a comfortable place to be, poncho man jarringly whirled me around, pointing apishly at a solitary figure.

"That's the girl you are always talking about, isn't it?" he bellowed. "Now is the time to talk to her."

I winced forcibly at that prospect. I wanted to be as carefree and fun loving as he was, but my intestines felt like wrung-out laundry at such moments. Pushing me toward her, his eager grin filled my spirit with temporary hope, just as it had lured me to abandon my dog-eared textbooks.

The girl's eyes darted energetically around the room, and I funneled my way through the crowd, hoping to catch them as I squirmed toward her. I soon got close enough that I could feel her exhaling against my chest, but words eluded me. From the length of the room, my buddy forcefully prodded me to take a chance, so I croaked the most interesting thing I could think of.

"Hi. I just got back from a summer in Paris. Have you been there?"

She shifted her stance to face me squarely and looked me over judiciously. My mind futilely reached out, clawing to retract the pompous statement from the air. While I half made to leave, a smile creased her face, and her voice pierced the humid atmosphere and thundering bass.

"I love Paris. I go there all the time!" she exclaimed.

My wall of nerves disintegrated. A cheesy grin plastered my face, and I caught poncho man's glance, hoping he could sense my victory. The minutes of conversation stretched into more minutes, and the talking points flowed like wine. I was elated until, like a tornado, a diminutive girl frantically willed her way toward us. The crowd parted, forfeiting any attempts to restrain her, and upon making it through, her focus narrowed on me. The veins in her eyes were tremors, conducting a more intense interrogation that made me keenly aware of my fault lines. She took in the messy hair, the smudged glasses, and the awful moustache as she whispered harshly into perfection's ear. After the longest second of my life, they turned on their heels and left through the crowd. The throng of people once again obliged, as if the course of events was preordained; the girls formed a growing procession toward the bathroom. Dumbfounded, I remained rooted to the spot, eyes fixed upon the black hole in the hope that they would return. Poncho man had warned me that girls got lost there forever, so I knew it was futile. From that moment, the mystery of the bathroom experience began to fester. I thought we had forged a great connection before it had all been swallowed up.

"Stick to the library, my son," my mum interjected. "Physics and chemistry hold mysteries that man can actually solve. You will never find the answer to the girls' bathroom. So go pack a healthy lunch now, sleep at a reasonable hour tonight, and I will talk to you this time tomorrow. Have a great day!"

September 18, 2011

16

Murder Leads to Guilt

EDITOR'S NOTE: PAUL'S very first short story, written at age sixteen while he was still in high school and published in the *International Journal for Teachers of English Writing Skills*, August 2006, special literary edition.

A body lay motionless on the floor, facedown with its legs spread out. The boys gasped in surprise and fear. It was a horrifying sight for them to see. A man was dead at their feet.

"Oh my God!" Ugo yelled. "Is that the chief?"

He pointed frantically at the still body and awaited an answer from his older brother. His brother did not reply though because he was in a state of shock.

The two brothers had broken into the house in an attempt to rob the village chief. They had been told that the chief was out of town, on vacation with his maid.

"What are we going to do? That is definitely the chief!" Ugo screamed. "Kelenna, I am scared...Answer me!"

Kelenna kicked the body gently, and it rolled onto its back. Foam was dripping from the chief's mouth, and his shirt was stained with sauce, from the food he must have been eating.

"Ugo, let's go," Kelenna muttered. He hauled their bags onto his back and tugged at his younger brother.

Kelenna was an imposing figure who loomed over everyone with his immense height. Ugo was usually very obedient, but this time he was just scared.

"Kele, we can't leave the body here. The chief's been murdered. Our fellow villagers will go crazy with outrage and shock."

"What do you propose we do then? We broke into this house, armed with picklocks and old rifles. Our goal was...is to rob this man." Kelenna paused and pondered for a moment. "Ah, we can't flee the scene until we rob it bare. We both know that we need to do this, so take this bag and start clearing this place out."

Ugo violently shook his head. He bit his upper lip as he trembled and stared up at his brother in timid defiance.

"You were right; we should leave, Kele," Ugo replied. He stumbled clumsily as he made to retreat, but the entrance to the room was blocked.

A robust man stood in the way with many men congregated behind him. His rusty gun was pointed at the dead body, and he looked in astonishment at the boys. There was a long period of silence as the man surveyed the scene.

Ugo started shaking in fear. Kelenna, on the other hand, appeared quite calm.

"What have you boys done!" the man bellowed.

Ugo jumped in fright, but Kelenna stood firm.

"You are coming with us."

The men flung the boys outside of the house and rained insults upon them. Ugo sobbed heavily as he lay sprawled out with his stomach on the sandy surface. The van doors slid open, and the men hauled them to their feet. Kelenna didn't struggle, but Ugo squirmed, kicked, and thrashed. The men quickly became frustrated because Ugo persisted in his struggle against them.

"You don't have to be gentle with him," the robust man snorted. His followers responded by stomping on Ugo. Everyone ignored Kelenna, to join in on the fun. He passively watched for a while as his brother's yelping mixed with the men's whoops of glee and amusement. Then, he grabbed their bags and dashed off, unnoticed.

Kelenna panted heavily as he banged on the door to his house. His father flung it open and gasped in feigned surprise.

"Where's your brother?" he asked.

"The 'Village Youth Brigade' took him. We are in trouble, Papa."

"Are you in a perilous situation?" he mocked. "What did you two troublemakers do now?"

Kelenna hesitated for a moment and gave his father a look that portrayed shame and regret. Then he explained to him what happened.

Once Kelenna had finished, his father turned away from him and flopped onto his sleeping mat.

"You want to fall asleep?" Kelenna cried.

"Yes," he moaned. He looked grumpily at Kelenna and closed his eyes.

"But everything is your fault. Ever since Ma died, you've been a lazy slob. We are struggling to make ends meet. We don't eat enough. We dropped out of school. Our clothes smell, and we are in debt. We borrow money from so many people even though you sold the family farm. What a paltry sum you received for that farm. You got duped by the chief, and now we have no source of income. You aren't even a true father," Kelenna cried.

He had not raised his voice, but his fists were clenched as tightly as a vice, and his eyes bulged so that they resembled frying pans.

"The Brigade will crash through that door any moment from now. I can see them out of the window. I don't know about you, but I am not bothering to run though," Papa John grumbled.

The leader of the Brigade was called Victor Nweze. His stocky frame was distinct, and he easily could be identified by it. He stood over Ugo, Kelenna, and Papa John with an expression of joy and relief. The three of them were lying on the floor of the little hut house they had been brought to, tied and gagged.

"We know you did not kill the chief. You couldn't have since we did." He chuckled.

Ugo was bruised and beaten, but he still writhed and squirmed as much as possible upon hearing these words.

"I am sorry, but you three are going to take the blame. You will all be executed tomorrow."

A woman sat crying quietly on the floor next to them. She stared at the ground as she wept and sobbed. Victor was very troubled by her sorrow and moved toward her.

"Everything will be fine tomorrow. He is gone, and he can't hurt you anymore," Victor whispered in an assuring manner.

The woman was fairly young, about twenty-three years of age. She shook her head slowly and looked up at Victor with her teary eyes. "This is not right, Victor. This is not the way it should be," she moaned.

"He deserved what he got. If he hadn't fallen 'ill,' you would have gone on a vacation with him. That would have been terrible, and you know it. He can't abuse you or use you anymore. You should be happy," Victor huffed.

The young woman stood up and left.

"Everything will be fine tomorrow!" Victor yelled after her.

Nothing turned out fine, though. The woman had disappeared the next day and so had Kelenna. Victor was shocked that Kelenna had ditched his brother yet again, but he was more concerned about the whereabouts of the woman.

He tried to remain optimistic. So they took Ugo and Papa John to the village square, where executions were done. Ugo was terrified, and Papa John peacefully slept throughout the journey.

At the village square, they found pandemonium and commotion. It was clear that someone had been executed. Victor jumped out of the van and barged through the crowd of people. He screamed in terror when he saw the limp body that hung from a noose. It was the woman—his woman.

"Why was this lady executed?" he growled.

"She poisoned the chief. She confessed to it herself," an old woman croaked.

The execution plans were swift. There was no remorse. Victor's heartbeat tripled its rate and pounded harder than ever before. He walked slowly back to the van and ordered his men to let Ugo and Papa John go.

"It's over," he muttered. "She's gone, and I didn't even tell her how much I loved her." Victor quickly grabbed a knife from his comrade's neck belt and sliced his own neck. Blood spewed out and gushed from his slit neck. He flopped to the ground and moaned for a while before life left his body.

Summer 2006

Blog Posts from *Looch & Leukemia: The Road to Recovery*

Looch, Lookemia, the Luxury Suite

Good day, Ladies and Gentlemen,

My name is Paul Uche, and I am a twenty-one-year-old from Nigeria. I go to the Massachusetts Institute of Technology, and I am a senior majoring in chemical engineering while minoring in creative writing.

On Tuesday, November 27, 2012, I was diagnosed with acute myeloid leukemia. (See Wikipedia, or ask a wide-eyed premed interested in oncology. Wikipedia might be faster.) I am now undergoing chemotherapy at Beth Israel and will be in the hospital for around a month. The road to recovery will be much longer than that, but as nice as hospital food, reclining beds, and brushing my teeth with green foam sticks are, I need to get back to running the mean streets of Cambridge and Boston.

For now, I just wanted to say hello and invite all of you to watch this page regularly. I have many plans for this page over the next couple of weeks and months.

To first state the obvious, I want my experience (ahem, my life) to keep on going: there are too many all-nighters left to pull, too much good food for me to taste, too much unreleased 2Pac for me to listen to, a new *Star Wars* trilogy coming, my rap career to kick-start, an energy crisis to resolve, and too many cool people for me to hang out with.

Apparently one out of seventy-seven men and women get diagnosed with leukemia in their lifetime. For now, I would say that you should do the best you can to support the cancer treatment infrastructures in your area. I will share some thoughts and ways to contribute, but for now, my one suggestion is to check out the Huntsman Cancer Institute at http://huntsmancancer.org/.

Thank you for your rapt attention. We will have fun. Stay tuned as there might be raps about leukemia.

Love,
Paul "Looch" Uche

November 30, 2012

I Respect Edward Cullen

Hello, everyone,

First of all I have to say that before today I was one of those men who failed to understand and thus disrespected what vampires go through. I am like Snoop Dogg. I like *True Blood*, but besides that, I have found this vampire faze to be drawn out and corny. I watched the first *Twilight* movie because some cute girls in my high school (shout out to ABA girls!) were going to watch it when it opened in theaters. (The Looch likes being around fun, cute girls. I don't need many other reasons to go out on adventures or to eat caramel popcorn at Shatti.) I also saw the third movie on television. I was bored enough to forget that these movies are not for me.

At any rate, while I think we need to move on to centurions or mole people or the descendants of Chewbacca for new fantastical movies, here are some ways in which I have come to respect Edward Cullen:

For one, the man lives a tough life because going outside during the day can be a pain. I mean, he will "shine bright like a diamond," if the sun's rays hit him. Rihanna did not do a good job of explaining to the world how detrimental this is to your health. I was disappointed at first when Edward did not explode like other vampires do, but I am going to be cooped up in this hospital room for at least a month. Not being able to go outside to take in the day sucks. One gold star to you, Edward!

What really makes Edward and me kindred spirits though is the fact that we ride around and get it even though our blood is subpar. Edward is a vampire (spoiler!), and vampires need to bite people's faces off or be nice guys and get blood substitutes in order to stay undead. I picture there being a vampire Trader Joe's for people who want to get blood responsibly. As for me, I have and will rely on blood transfusions. I have had an infusion of both platelets and red blood cells. That really just means that I listen to 50 Cent while a bag of blood drips slowly into my chest. My blood-cell counts are all low because of both the cancer and the chemotherapy; I will quickly run through the implications:

White blood cells: they provide immunity and help me fight off infection and disease. My white-blood-cell count is low, so without God and medicine, I am screwed.

Red blood cells: they help transport oxygen throughout my body. My red-blood-cell count is low, so my energy levels dip as they do. In short, I am becoming anemic.

Platelets: they help clot my blood. For completeness, you should know that my platelets are low. I needed the platelet transfusion ASAP because if I get cut, I will bleed more than the bad guys did in *Kill Bill*. I am going to take a picture of the kind of toothbrush I have to use on a daily basis as an extra precaution. I would post it here, but for now I am lazy.

All in all, I realize that I am not all that different from Edward Cullen. I am just trying to live a rewarding life, maybe meet the girl of my dreams and eventually give her an uncomfortable pregnancy (in eight to ten years, barring accidents) while feeding off of other people's generous blood donations.

If you ever get the chance to donate blood, please consider doing so. Transfusions are helping me, and they help a lot of other people.

I am Team Edward, and I love all of you,
Paul "Looch" Uche

December 1, 2012

November 26, 2012

Hello, everyone,

Today is an interesting day for me in that it has now been a week since I first saw the blood results that pointed to me having cancer. At about this time last Monday (November 26), I was staring at a computer screen, wrapping my head around what it meant to have such low blood-cell counts across the board.

A week on, I want to start by thanking God that I went to the hospital last Monday. I had been feeling a little bit feverish the Friday before but did not think much of it. My good friend Joao gave me a steady stream of ibuprofen, which helped me function. I did most of my homework on Saturday in between napping. (So I did problem sets during the onset of cancer. I dare you to try and procrastinate work now…just kidding.) My premed, fellow-chemical-engineering, vice-presidential, newly naturalized-American buddy, David, checked my temperature, which was 102 degree Fahrenheit. (Google can translate this to Celsius.) On Sunday I had the shakes at times. I sweated. I had a pounding headache, and my 102-degree temperature persisted. Joao kept up the supply of ibuprofen, and I started wearing nothing but boxers and a poncho made out of a blanket that had a hole torn in the middle. I wish I had pictures. I remember telling Mike on the way to UBurger, "I have a temperature of one hundred two degrees Fahrenheit, but I am such a thug that it ain't nothing." Now, Mike and I are indeed thugs. Just check the records, but once again I am glad that I woke up and went to MIT Medical the next day.

On this one-week anniversary of sorts, I also have an overwhelming desire to be outside. I want to climb trees, get in snow fights, swim right after eating, play basketball in Tims (Timberland boots), parkour, ride my bike down hills, get out a Slip 'N Slide, sit on my stoop, grill dead animals, ghost ride the whip, get a tan, toss a disc, try golf, and walk around with a boom box on my shoulder.

While I am out of commission, please do any and all of the things I just mentioned. I have more suggestions if the list above feels incomplete to you. Also, remember to take care of yourselves. Part of being young is feeling like you are untouchable, but sometimes the smart thing to do is to get looked at and after.

The last thing I would like to say for now is that my biggest takeaway this week has been that leukemia has not and cannot take anything away from me. I still have all of my hopes and dreams. I have more people who love and care about me than I can keep track of. I have God by my side and my whole life ahead of me. I will walk down the street with a boom box on my shoulder blasting "Thug Mentality" by Bone Thugs-N-Harmony.

Love,
Paul "Looch" Uche

December 3, 2012

Endings

The bed let out its trademark mechanical squeal as it lurched forward and pulled me upright with it. Now cajoled to work, I pounded away at my tired laptop to finish off one last report. My eyes were heavy; falling asleep under the bed's white blankets was an alluring idea. The nurse brought in a cup of coffee to keep me going. The caffeine teamed up with a unit of red blood, which trickled into my chest, to ward off the anemia.

That Wednesday morning was a microcosm of my semester. I had undergone nearly six months of doctors' appointments, blood draws, and transfusions to beat back the effects of consolidation chemotherapy. I had come through being hospitalized for twenty-two days during the semester as well. In the end, I had successfully lived the life of a cancer patient striving to become a college graduate. Given my circumstances, Wednesday was a weirdly poetic way to end my undergraduate career.

Two weeks ago, on May 16, 2013, I handed in the last of my work. I felt like a rundown car battery, like a boxer whom had been battered for twelve rounds, but also like I had won on the scorecards.

And indeed I had.

I am glad that I decided to go through with finishing school. My coursework kept me focused and occupied. I think things would have been a lot harder if I fell out of the routine of going to lectures, talking to classmates about science, checking out the girl in the row ahead of me, and rushing to meet deadlines. I swapped libraries for waiting rooms and hospital beds, and it was worth it. I am thankful that it was all possible. That I managed it is not a testament to me. I have to thank my professors, my department, my school, my classmates, my friends, my family, and God. I need to ask someone with a SAG card how they go around thanking all of the people who helped them with their accomplishments.

Now, two weeks on, I am starting my last round of chemotherapy. My final dose will be on Tuesday. Unlike after season three of *Arrested Development*, I hope and pray that this is indeed the end. I will get some rest and relaxation during the summer and peddle my newly minted degree to get a job. Eventually.

Best regards,
Paul "Looch" Uche

May 30, 2013

Beginnings

Hello, everyone,

This blog has been an incredibly fun experience in the midst of the trying, weird, painful, insightful time that has been my battle with leukemia. Being able to share my thoughts with all of you has been a blessing, and I thank you for supporting me and this outlet. For now, this is the last long-form piece I will write. Appropriately and in continued admiration of Edward Cullen, I am getting a red blood transfusion while I type.

The questions that loomed largest back in November centered around what my life would look like in six months. How healthy would I be? Where would I be with school? Fast-forwarding to the present, I am in remission and have undergone all of my consolidation treatment. I will become neutropenic one more time, don the pink mask as a result, and visit Beth Israel for follow-ups ever so many days a week. With all that being said, my health has reached a big milestone. Furthermore, I have come to a landmark moment as a gentleman and a scholar: I can now officially call myself a college graduate.

As such, while Kanye West and I are both esteemed rappers, only one of us came out of college with a degree. He can try to comfort himself with his money, fame, awards, kilts, celebrity baby mama, and big brother. I walked, shook President Reif's hand, and quivered under part of a space blanket because it rained on us throughout commencement.

The risk of hypothermia aside, I am ecstatic that I graduated with all of my peers and friends with my family in attendance. If this blog was made into a movie, me walking away from Killian Court, with the MIT dome in the background and degree under my arm, would be its final scene. I can't decide whether I could get over the corniness of playing "I Love College" by Asher Roth during the end credits though. Ah well, that is the song I think I would go with, shame be damned.

I still ask a lot of questions about what will happen next. Now that I have graduated, I am technically unemployed. I have not thought about a job this entire year. I will be in Boston until mid-August, but I don't know where I will live long term. I plan on doing a lot of creative writing this summer, but I don't know what the ultimate writing project will look like, how many millions I will make from it, or how else I will fill my time (getting reacquainted with alcohol probably—that is, undoing all of the detoxing I have done).

The funny thing is that until now, my only responsibility in life, especially after dodging the bullet of teen pregnancy, has been to learn as much as possible. I nerded it up and sacrificed becoming a professional soccer player in order to get as good of an education as possible. I was not the coolest kid in middle school because of my commitment to my academic hustle. Now that that is all done with, I have to confront the fact that I have no idea how a 401(k) works, among other things. I might not be prepared to live like a real person.

I am grateful though that I get the chance to struggle through adult life. I am also overwhelmingly appreciative of the love and support you have given to me. Cancer is hard, but I never walked alone, and I don't even support Liverpool FC. I will have to deal with cancer in some way for years to come, and while that is a bit nerve-racking, I accept it. I would like to say, as scary as this illness is, it does not need to dictate, define, or drag down your life. The human spirit is strong, and hope reigns supreme. Life is a funny beast that throws a lot of curveballs at you. Cancer is a harsh example of this. People ask, "How do you stay positive through all of this?" The way I see it is that when I wake up, my dilemma exists whether I like it or not. My situation is crappy, but it will only be worse if I kowtow to the cards I have been dealt. I don't have superpowers, and I am not happy all the time, because I am not a Teletubby, but I have influence over every given day. I can decide to smile and enjoy the wonderful people and environment around me. I am more acutely aware of how important it is to embrace what you have.

The mushy truth is that I choose life and I choose love.

So, a final cheer to new beginnings.

Love,
Paul "Looch" Uche

June 12, 2013

The Sequel

Hello again,

As many of you know, my leukemia is unfortunately back.

I moved to Toronto last Sunday and had a final biopsy prior to that on August 6 at Beth Israel. The bone-marrow biopsy was the final step in my summer of follow-ups.

I was just about ready to move on with my life and had even convinced myself that I could pretend to adore hockey. Instead, I was told the night after my biopsy that there were abnormalities in my marrow, which were confirmed to be emergent cancer cells on Friday. At the time, 20 percent of my bone marrow was filled with leukemia. That number is now above 50 percent and growing. I have not started any treatment yet, a lot of things are in the air, but I know that I am going to need a bone-marrow transplant. My body has not started breaking down yet, but I will need to start with a round of chemotherapy very soon. I always knew that a relapse was possible, but it is a bummer that it has happened so soon. I was healthy again in the month of July, which was just in time to bring it back and enjoy the Fourth, among other things. :)

A lot has happened in a short period of time. I hope to write faithfully to keep you all up to date on how things are going (especially as I have transferred my care to the Princess Margaret Hospital in Toronto). Shipping out of Boston was stressful because it meant leaving my friends and the medical team at Beth Israel that I both appreciate and feel comfortable with.

This is a tough time, but your support means everything, so I am optimistic and know that we will have some fun again.

Love,
Paul "Looch" Uche
PS: I might have to boycott Taylor Swift because quoting her by saying, "We are never ever getting back together," did me no good. In fact, I want my money back!

August 15, 2013

Making a Difference

Hello, everyone,

One of the things that has been awesome to see is the number of bone-marrow drives that have been organized all over the place. There is a Facebook group that my brother started, which aggregates a lot of cheek-swab opportunities. I personally wanted to touch on a couple of drives:

This Saturday, there will be a bone-marrow drive at MIT. There are also upcoming drives in Toronto, Houston, and Atlanta, and people have been getting swabbed in clinics in Dubai.

The response has been humbling and exciting. I am happy that this experience has motivated people to make a difference. Truly, ordering a swab kit in the mail or taking part in a drive changes lives.

I feel this acutely as I wait for a donor to emerge. Without a donor in place, I am in limbo right now. I receive a range of drugs that work like an elaborate Band-Aid, but I can't progress in my treatment without the means to undergo a transplant. Waiting is a strange feeling, but it is good to know that a lot is going on around me.

Best,
Paul "Looch" Uche

October 3, 2013

The Donor

Hello, everyone,

My bone-marrow search took quite a while. At a certain point, I stopped asking for frequent updates because I felt like the kid in the back of the car yelling, "Are we there yet?" As with many things, patience and faith are what I had to rely on.

I can now say that I have an unrelated donor and shared the following as my Facebook status yesterday:

> I would like to thank you for your response to my relapse. You raised awareness for blood cancer patients, helped organize and participate in bone-marrow drives, and voluntarily mailed in cheek-swab kits. Because of people like you, I have a donor and can, in time, get a transplant. An important takeaway is that we have seen how we can affect people's lives. I am humbled that you rallied on my behalf, but what excites me is everyone we potentially helped. With that, thanks again and keep that drive to help others.

Being the figurehead of a campaign was a strange and rewarding experience. I had to get used to seeing my face across Facebook, but it obviously meant that people were rallying around me.

I am still trying to get healthy enough for a clinical transplant, so there is still a lot of work to do.

Best regards,
Paul "Looch" Uche

November 5, 2013

Songs

Somewhere in Immigrant America

Nigeria is all up in my blood stream,
But anything can happen in America
Unless you want bills passed by senators.
So we are out here chasing the same dream.
They think we'll do bad like Erykah,
So they want to raise the walls a little higher.
I just want a higher education,
So I can raise this world a little higher.
I have trust issues with the system
Because my politicians never listened.
I believe over here it is different,
So I subscribe to your vision.
I have an elephant but I ain't Republican.
They're looking at my passport like I'm ruffian
Like I am rushing in to steal all of your positions,
But let's focus on some real afflictions.
Yo—I want to see real equality.
Yo—we have to wash away hypocrisy.
No—it doesn't work, all of these projects.
So—honestly it's a work in progress.
I see you bleeding red, white, and blue.
I see you fighting for what's fair and true.
It's hard to have all this power,
But somebody has to come through.
Now back home I seem more alien.
Play *Watch the Throne*, listen to all these aliens.

You might be wondering how I speak so smoothly.
I am wondering how we forgot Fela Kuti.
And people risk everything all to be here,
Even if it puts them square in your crosshairs.
And me, I am still putting work in
'Cause somewhere in America, Miley is still twerking.

Burger and Shake

I'm running, screaming, "Yes, I can sir."
Though I don't have all the answers,
I'm both human and dancer.
So I try to hit like a lancer.

Verse
A new diagnosis, I am so ill and ill,
So my focus now is love and bigger thrills.
I dream of riding my bike to my fratcastle
With the balls to fight I feel like Sam Cassel.
Some claim that I am young and reckless,
Blue gown, brown socks, where is my necklace?
I down room service for breakfast.
I feel blessed with the skills to kill a record.
Aiming for the Hall like shots at Arsenio,
I step inside the booth to bring you brand new material.
I am living proof that you can be fly without the legroom,
A cut above, like a suffering head wound.
We are ripping beats, working outside of the system.

Chorus
And what I want in the worst way
Ha! In the worst way
Is to breakout, get a burger and shake
And walk, one time I will say,
What I want, what I want
is to break out, get a burger and shake.

Verse

I must confess something that you ought to know
I am changing up the recipe like Dominos.
And while I stress that I don't have a lot of foes,
I am on point like models in tall stilettos.
So up a rung, I run my tongue for exercise,
And challenge anyone who wants to come and step inside.
I am a mac while these guys are just side orders.
I want it all like hoarders, get out your camcorders.
They are waiting on me like a new Andre Young track,
So I bust through, cause a racquet like Dunlap.
A fun fact is that it's now time for my comeback.
And when I cross the finish line, I'll still run laps,
'Cause this feels like a great fit, threads top designer.
A reminder: I am so ready to be the top headliner,
So trapping me behind a border
Is borderline insane.
If I don't fit in, I will change all the dimensions.
I have a lot of doctors giving sweet prescriptions.
Mine is simple: rise above all afflictions.

(*Chorus*)

Verse

I want to make it rain till it rainbows,
Blow up big like Notorious parade floats.
Glorious, I am so far from on hiatus.

I am still fiending to dominate your playlist.
Bald like Bruce Willis, so badass.
I am in this, more than that nerd in your math class.
I mash the gas to keep on contending,
With flow, beats, soul, and invention.
I am in the throws now of crazy cabin fever.
Some days I feel lazy, some days I feel G'd up.
A poor slice of luck like grabbing stale pizza,
But I am not having that, so we kick it like FIFA.
And I might start free-falling Tom Petty,
But tonight I feel strong, beyond ready.
I ball like a monster, ask Halle Berry,
So we are celebrating and sipping, yelling hallelujah.

Thank you all for your attention.
I don't know if I mentioned this, but I'm here to take
over the whole world.
It's really hard to do that on hospital food.
They are taking care of me though, but don't get in my
the row.
It's Paulo Chuck! Burgers and shakes: I love them; I
need them; I feel them.
Let's go!

Blue

Verse
And they might see some pant saggers,
Deluded tongue wagger after thought rappers,
Instead of young masters, making moves like Jagger.
So far from slackers except on your radio,
Stacks getting fatter.
Maybe we should have been practical.
Stayed inside our lane, kept away from your avenues,
But we knew that all of this could be magical.
So we found a way, now our voices are so powerful.
They used to say that your raps just cause a racket.
Now we are getting chosen/picked first in everybody's
brackets.
The top dogs, better sew the C atop our jackets.
When it comes to heat, we are UPS because we pack it.
And I can't sit around thinking "maybe one day."
Let me get fresh and then I will meet you on the runway.
Step into the world, man I just got my diploma.
Best believe I am looking for success and its aroma.

Chorus
We are at a crosswords with so much we can do,
And I know that you will explode, I believe in you.
They might say that you don't belong, but that just
ain't true.
At the end of the day we are so fly, all I see is Blue.

Verse

Now, I blast my own tunes, I am a narcissist.
No need to make room, I am already a part of this.
Showing gratitude to the men that fathered this,
Now I'm laying down my own plans like an architect.
Late to the scene but never tardy.
In love with life, I bring cheer and Bacardi.
Tonight you do you and I'll do me,
And we'll kill it to the same degree.
Never feel like a second-class citizen,
Entering the real and it has them all quivering.
I make sure my chain hangs baby but never my head.
I make sure the beats bang baby as I get this bread
Sorry, yo, there is just no restraining us.
A taxi flow, because soon they will be hailing us.
Yo can go HAM or remain miscellaneous, anonymous.
Me blowing up was far from spontaneous.

(*Chorus*)

Verse

I wonder where I will be in ten years.
I wonder if they will be my Eminem years,
Whether I will shed tears or maybe shed fears, peers.
I am trying to get ahead here.
Though I am twenty-two, with a bunch that I am figuring,
Trying to find my shot, in my high-tops I am pivoting.

I feel like my whole life I have been simmering,
And now I am boiling hot in pole positioning.
And I see these rappers getting punked in here like Johnny Rotten.
I just hope that they fall for me like it is autumn.
A pack of ramen in my belly and a lot of fire,
You want a jam that is hot in here?
You are preaching to the choir.

(*Chorus*, twice)
We are at a crossroads with so much we can do.
And I know that you will explode, I believe in you.
They might say that you don't belong, but that just ain't true.
At the end of the day we are so fly, all I see is Blue.
And while they say that us as stars man is a façade,
I am not shook, I look around at entourage.
On the job pound for pound, we can take the battle scars,
Hustled hard since the schoolyard so now the world is ours.

Author Biography

PAUL UCHECHUKWU UCHE passed away June 19, 2014, in Toronto, Canada. The young writer was twenty-three years old.

Born in Warri, Nigeria, Uche traveled extensively throughout his short life, spending time in Nigeria, the Netherlands, Malaysia, Oman, the United States, and Canada. After graduating from the American-British Academy International Baccalaureate program in Oman, Uche chose to study at the Massachusetts Institute of Technology in Boston, where he majored in chemical engineering with a minor in creative writing.

During his time at the American-British Academy, Uche played on the basketball, volleyball, and soccer teams, winning the Athlete of the Year Award. He was an executive member of the ABA Students Against Prejudice club and won the prestigious ABA Citizenship Award.

Uche's first short story, "Murder Leads to Guilt," was published in the August 2006 edition of the International Journal for Teachers of English Writing Skills.

Author at just under two years in The Netherlands – January 1993

At just over two years in Miri, Malaysia, 1993

Stepping off to pre-school for the first time in Miri, Malaysia.

First year in boarding school at Loyola Jesuit
College, Abuja, Nigeria. 2002

A cache of academic awards from the American British
Academy (ABA), Muscat, Sultanate of Oman, 2008.

Author (left) a proud Nigerian, with his brother Bernie,
at the Africa Day event in Muscat, May 2009.

A very happy and healthy MIT Chemical Engineering
student, Cambridge Massachussets, 2011

The Dashing MIT senior, 2012

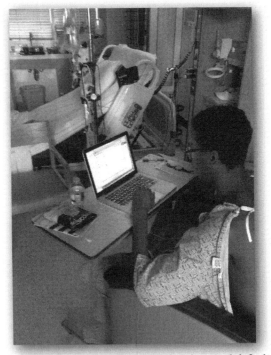

Illness suddenly and rudely intruded, but Paul defied
it till the very end.
Doing serious work in his hospital room at Beth Isreal
Deaconess Medical Centre, Boston Massachussets, 2012.

Against all the odds, Paul graduates with his peers (June 7, 2013) to
become The Triple Threat:
Musician, Writer, Engineer.

Author with family at the graduation ceremony, June 7 2013.

44713255R00100

Made in the USA
Charleston, SC
04 August 2015